THE WORLD OF

SUPERSAURS

TEMPLE OF THE SAURS

UNLEASH THE SAURS!

BOOKS:

Raptors of Paradise
The Stegosorcerer
Clash of the Tyrants
Temple of the Saurs
Available from all places good books are sold.

APP:

Download the free Supersaurs app to experience more
and see the saurs come to life.

Available free on Apple from iTunes App Store
and on Android from Google Play Store.

WEBSITE:

Head to the Supersaurs website for bonus material,
news, events and more!

www.supersaurs.com

THE WORLD OF
SUPERSAURS
TEMPLE OF THE SAURS

JAY JAY BURRIDGE

First published in Great Britain in 2019 by
Supersaurs
80-81 Wimpole Street, London, W1G 9RE
www.supersaurs.com

Text and illustrations copyright © Supersaurs Limited, 2019
Illustrations by Chris West & Jay Jay Burridge

A CIP catalogue record for this book is available from the British Library.

ISBN: 978–1–786–96816-6

1 2 3 4 5 6 7 8 9 10

Typeset in Adobe Jenson by Perfect Bound Ltd
Printed and bound by Page Bros., Norwich

Supersaurs is an imprint of Bonnier Zaffre,
part of Bonnier Books UK
www.bonnierbooks.co.uk

*For Mouse, Bear and Fox
and all the other creatures in my life.*

Golfo de México

TAMPICO

OIL

VERACRUZ

HIDALGO

PACHUCA

PULQUE

PYRAMIDS

MEXICO CITY

TLAXCALA

EL POPO 5,395 MT.

CHOLULA 300 CHURCHES

NECAXA

JALAPA

FAMOSA CERVEZA

ORIZABA 5,700 MT.

MALTRATA

VERACRUZ

OIL

PUEBLA

OAXACA

MITLA RUINS

OAXACA

ITSMO DE TEHUANTEPEC

COPAINA

CINTALAPA

SALINA CRUZ

ACAPULCO BAY

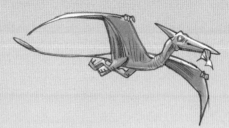

I

Grace and Franklin

~ two halves of the same thing ~

**Koto Lama, Wokan, the Islands of Aru,
Maluku Province of Eastern Indonesia, 1921**

Franklin Kingsley woke with a start in a tangle of old fishing nets strung out to dry under the hut. His well-used hammock had finally given way, abruptly ending his mid-morning nap.

'Frank, are you awake?' asked Grace from inside.

'I am now,' Franklin replied, rolling out of the shade and onto the hot sand.

'Good.' Grace came out and smiled at her husband. 'I'm almost done here – shouldn't we be heading off to meet Lambert soon?'

Franklin stared at his watch and then quickly shook himself down. 'Yes, better get a move on.' He untied the hammock and inspected it. 'I'll treat myself to a new one at the general store before we set off.'

'Give me a moment. Carter will need feeding and I just want to let this watercolour dry.' Grace placed her sketchbook in the scorching sunlight.

'What are you painting – Carter?'

'Yes,' Grace said. 'I was just colouring in some old sketches while he sleeps.' She admired her handiwork and dabbed at it to check whether it was safe yet to close the pages. The little squares of pigment had already dried out in the heat.

'You all packed?' Franklin asked. 'Remember – we have to travel light.' He picked up his kit bag, and, finding it a smidge too heavy, reached in to take out his half-filled leather-bound journal containing all his notes of the past few months. He flicked through the pages, stopping on his last entry and paused as he read through it again.

'I'll use my small notebook on this short trip and keep this safe here,' he said to himself before tucking it inside the old fishing satchel his best man, Theodore, had given him. He then packed the bag into the upright trunk they were leaving behind.

Grace swabbed her wet brush on a rag and folded up her tin of watercolours. She returned it with the brushes and her large sketchbook to the trunk.

Carter gurgled and waved his arms at his father. 'There, there, little man,' Franklin cooed.

'Hand him over,' Grace said, taking a seat in Jara's rocking chair. 'Tell me about this guide you found.'

'Strange thing is, *he* found *me*.' Franklin paused. 'He walked straight up to me and said, "I can take you to find what you're looking for." Just like that.'

Grace scrunched up her face. 'And you think he can? Sounds like he's just after money.'

Franklin shook his head. 'He's not charging us.'

'Really? Well, how did he know you were after a guide?' Grace quizzed her husband.

Franklin shrugged his shoulders. 'When I asked about the saurs we might see he gave this big red smile and said, "Let's find that rainbow you're looking for first."'

'Rainbow – that's not a Raptor of Paradise I've ever heard of,' Grace remarked.

'Exactly what I said,' Franklin replied. 'And then he said it's a tree.'

Grace froze. 'Why would he say that?' she uttered. 'How does he know we're looking for a temple tree?'

'Like I said, *he* found *me*.' Franklin shrugged again. 'It's most odd. I think we have to go along with him. It's not the first time we've run into this sort of coincidence or luck, is it?' Franklin raised his eyes at Grace.

'You're right. Should we be taking Lambert, though?

This expedition is getting rather large, isn't it?'

'Lambert's harmless,' Franklin replied. 'He's just awfully keen.'

'But you hardly know him,' Grace protested. 'Are you sure you can trust him? He's no Theo, you know.'

'I don't see why not,' Franklin answered. 'I don't see the harm in it. He seems an interesting chap. I'm rather glad he's decided to come along – it's been good having someone to talk to about the real reason we're here.'

'You haven't told him *everything*, have you?'

Franklin sighed. 'I may have told him a bit too much,' he conceded. 'Not everything, though – not about the Saurman temple we're looking for.'

'What if we don't find it, Franklin?' Grace asked, as Carter let out a milky burp.

Franklin smiled. 'Don't worry – we'll find the temple, and hopefully some of those elusive Raptors of Paradise you're dying to see. I have no doubts. Say,' he continued, 'have you finished that letter for Bea? I'll take it into the Post Office before we leave.'

'I just have to sign it,' Grace murmured with a sigh. 'I do miss her so.' She gazed lovingly into her baby boy's contented face as she fed him. 'She will have grown up – I'll barely recognise her by the time we return!'

'She's in good hands with Bunty,' Franklin assured her. 'They'll both be quite surprised to hear about Carter! I hope she likes having a baby brother!'

'Surprises are the best part of life,' Grace retorted with a smile. 'You never know what's round the corner. It keeps you on your toes.'

+ + +

As Franklin was loading their bags onto the juvenile kylo loaned to them, Jara knocked on the door of the hut. 'I have that feather you asked for, the one to send to your daughter,' she said.

'Oh, Jara – it's wonderful, thank you,' Grace replied. 'Bea will absolutely love it. Perhaps one day she'll see the owner of this feather, a Raptor of Paradise, for herself. I know I can't wait.'

'Grace,' Jara ventured, 'I don't mean to be nosy, but I was outside the hut mending a fishing net earlier, and I heard you mention that you're looking for a temple in the jungle. Is that right?'

'Don't apologise, Jara.' Grace smiled. 'I can hear the people on the other side of the village!'

'It's just that there aren't any temples on this island,' Jara said in a concerned voice. 'And this feather is the closest you might get to catching a glimpse of a Raptor of Paradise – must you go?'

Grace tried to find the words to explain. 'I don't know; it feels like it's our destiny.' She shrugged and smiled.

'Well, do as you must,' Jara said. 'I'll be here when you come back, and I hope you find what you're looking for. I brought you that wrap for the baby as well. I'll show you how to use it to carry the baby after you've finished.'

'Thank you, Jara. I don't know what I would have done without your help,' Grace said.

As Jara bustled out of the door Grace looked at the colourful feather with a sigh. Soon she would be home and cuddling both of her children. Telling Bea all about Carter would have to wait. For now she just signed:

> *Always   and   forever,   your loving mother,*
>
> *Grace xxx*

She tucked the feather into the envelope and sealed it shut.

❖ ❖ ❖

Jara helped Grace adjust the wrap inside which Carter lay with folded limbs, while Franklin tightened the last strap on the kylo.

'Junti –' Franklin tugged on the lead – 'you've eaten enough – there are plenty more ferns to eat in the jungle.'

The short walk round the headland to Koto Baru, the new town, took ages. The kylo kept stopping to eat and Grace kept making small adjustments to the wrap carrier that was holding baby Carter.

As they approached the town they came across huts and people. Eventually they rested in the shade of a large wooden sign next to the dock and were soon approached by two men.

'The lovely Mrs Kingsley,' Lambert purred, bowing to Grace.

'Viscount Knútr,' Grace responded, 'it's a pleasure.'

'Please, just call me Lambert.' He smiled. 'May I introduce Mr Christian Hayter, an associate of mine with extensive experience handling saurs. He will be a very suitable guide for our trip into the jungle.'

'Pleased to meet you,' Franklin said, shaking Hayter's hand.

'Same,' Hayter replied, and nodded at Grace.

'That's quite a fearsome instrument you've got there, Mr Hayter,' Grace remarked, noticing that Hayter's other hand remained fast upon a bullhook tucked into his belt.

'Comes in handy,' Hayter replied gruffly.

'I'm afraid we won't be needing your services, however, Mr Hayter,' Franklin said. 'I appreciate the help, Lambert, but we already have a guide. He's called Kunava – a local man who knows the interior of the island well.'

'Excellent, excellent,' Lambert gushed. 'Well, how about we use both? Your Mr Kunava can show us the way, and Mr Hayter here can keep us out of trouble. What do you say?'

Franklin smiled politely. 'We won't be getting into trouble.'

'All the same . . .' Lambert insisted, equally politely,

and with just as broad a smile. 'Grace – I trust you'll be joining us?' Lambert beamed in Grace's direction.

'Of course,' Grace replied. 'I'm looking forward to it.'

'She insists!' Franklin laughed.

'And your boy – little Carter?' Lambert persisted.

'I'd never leave him,' Grace replied simply.

Franklin sighed. He knew how demanding such a trip could be and wished his headstrong wife would take the time to rest, but he knew how important this trip was to her.

'Of course, of course.' Lambert smiled at Grace, then turned to Franklin. 'Even more reason to use two guides. The more the merrier – eh, Hayter?'

Hayter shuffled and crossed his arms. 'Whatever you say, boss.'

'No need to call me that – we're all friends here.' Lambert gave Hayter a swift glance. 'Now, where's that native of yours, Franklin?' he said shortly, looking around. 'Perhaps he overslept?'

'Kunava will be meeting us at the treeline,' Franklin assured him. 'If you don't mind, we'll swing by the Post Office on our way out. My daughter's going to love getting her letter.'

'Of course,' Lambert said.

As Franklin moved off alongside the kylos with Grace and Carter by his side the Viscount hung back with Hayter and in a low voice whispered, 'Let's worry about the Dutchman after our trip.'

Hayter nodded.

'Good,' the Viscount said. 'And make sure that letter never leaves the island.'

THE DUTCH EAST INDIA COMPANY
WELCOME TO KOTO BARU
WOKAN ISLAND OF THE ARU ISLANDS
MALUKU PROVINCE   EASTERN INDONESIA

HOME OF THE EXOTIC RAPTORS OF PARADISE

PLEASE RESPECT THE WILDLIFE. TAKE CAUTION WHEN
ENTERING THE JUNGLE AND NEVER REST UNDER COCONU
THE GATHERING AND TRADING IN LOCAL SPICE IS B
UPON ARRIVAL FROM THE GOVERNORS OFFICE

2

Arrival by Land

~ Budge ~

'Move!' Bea urged, her voice weary. 'I don't care if you're tired, or hungry, or hot, or just fed up – you HAVE to budge!' She leant against the brachio's side and heaved. She might as well have been trying to move a wall. 'I'm all of those things too, but we can't stay here,' she went on. 'We're nearly there. Just an afternoon's walk.' She patted the juvenile saur's nose. 'Please,' she tried.

'What's the problem, Bea?' Theodore said, as he and Carter pulled up beside her on Buster. 'First you race on ahead, then you stop. Why did you get off? Is he giving you trouble?'

Bea shot Theodore a frustrated look. 'He's not used to being ridden, that's all,' she said defensively. 'He's only young, and he's spent his whole life chained up unable to go further than ten feet in any direction, so now he wants to go everywhere all at once.'

'Or nowhere,' Theodore said. 'What do you think, Carter, can you try to get him to behave?'

Carter shrugged. 'No,' he replied. 'But he's happy. And Buster likes him, too.'

Theodore looked up and down the dusty road. There wasn't much traffic. They'd travelled down to Mexico in style on a series of trains, but recently their luck had changed and that was no longer an option. Bea had acquired her own form of transport in the form of the brachio, however, which at least allowed them all to ride the last leg of the journey. Unfortunately Bea's ride was about as stubborn as she was.

'We have to get into town by nightfall,' Theodore reminded them. 'Lambert's expecting us. Bea – why don't you try singing to him? That seems to get his attention.'

The rumble of a truck approaching caused the young brachio to turn his head. A cloud of dust followed it, and as it drew closer they could see that the open back was filled with men. There was no way all of them were going to be able to fit onto the same road, so either they hurried along, or tried to squeeze to one side to let it pass. Unfortunately Buster didn't fit into tight spaces too readily, and the brachio didn't care to. The jungle pressed close on both sides of the road, presenting an impenetrable wall of trees and undergrowth.

Carter and Theodore urged Buster ahead to find a good passing place as the truck sounded its horn.

'Come on,' Bea pleaded, kicking in her heels, the panic rising in her voice as the truck approached. 'Come on, BUDGE!' she shouted to no avail.

Suddenly the crack of a rifle sounded as a warning shot was fired into the air. The trees rustled madly in response as hundreds of birds took flight at once. Thankfully they weren't the only things to decide a quick getaway was in order. The brachio broke out of his stupor and bolted.

'About time!' Bea muttered, hanging on for dear life. She quickly spotted Buster and the boys, and a sharp tug on the brachio's reins successfully brought him next to them tucked into a gap in the trees. As the truck roared past a few of the men tossed papers in the air. Carter caught one as it floated down. On it was a crude print of a black skull and the words *VIVA LA REVOLUCIÓN!*

'Rebels,' Theodore said uneasily. 'I had heard rumours of them making a stronghold in this area. We'd do best to avoid them. Let's get out of here.'

The massive brachio once again refused to move.

'You don't have to convince me,' Bea huffed. 'It's this saur who needs motivating. Don't be scared,' she said softly now, and stroked his neck. 'But you do need to move. Come on, budge.'

The brachio seemed to have a change of heart and moved on.

'He likes that name,' Carter said.

'What name?' Bea asked.

Carter smiled. 'Budge.'

* * *

They arrived at the Hotel Espléndido at dusk. Carter and Bea remained outside while Theodore went to register at the reception desk. Mérida was a small town with a central square near the coast, and locals were back about their business after taking a siesta in the heat of the day. Plenty of people stopped to stare at Buster, as they had never seen a Black Tyrant in this part of the world. Carter and Bea refreshed themselves at the fountain in the square, and Buster sent a small crowd of curious children running when he shook out his feathers, sending sprinkles everywhere.

Eventually Theodore came out, but he had bad news. 'I'm afraid there's been a mix-up,' he told them. 'Lambert isn't here – he had to go away on business, they said. The hotel manager wouldn't let Lambert reserve our room, but he did arrange to accommodate Buster, whom they think is an exotic allosaur, in the stables.' Theodore paused. 'Please don't let them know he's a Dwarf Tyrant,' he said under his breath. 'I get the feeling tyrants aren't much liked here.'

'Can't we just pay extra to have them make room for Budge?' Carter asked.

'Unfortunately he could not accommodate two saurs, as Lambert had only told him about Buster,' Theodore said, sighing. 'In fact, he was quite amazed we had one. So we're going to have to make do until Lambert returns or find somewhere else for us and the saurs to stay.'

'When will Lambert be back?' asked Bea, who'd been rather looking forward to a nice bath.

'They don't know, I'm afraid. He left instructions for us to check at the desk every day at noon. In the meantime we're supposed to enjoy the delights of the town and equip ourselves with anything we need for our journey into the jungle to find the lost city – ropes and so on. But unfortunately Lambert didn't pay for the rooms before he left, so . . .' Theodore trailed off looking miserable and glanced momentarily at Bea. 'But we don't have any money left after –' He stopped himself from saying more. 'The manager asked for the first night up front. I tried to explain Lambert would pay on his return.' He shook his head and sighed.

'I, for one, will be happy to make do,' announced Bea stoically. 'There has to be a place that's more friendly with less rules.'

'And food,' Carter added. 'Buster and I are hungry.'

'Well, Budge and I aren't,' Bea shrugged. 'He's a herbivore and has plenty to eat, and I have my *chapulines*. It's not my fault you refuse to eat them.'

Theodore winced. 'I can't eat insects.'

'I can't eat cooked insects,' Carter said. 'Fresh are much better for you.'

'Speaking of which, Bea,' Theodore noted, 'perhaps your brachio has eaten enough.'

They all turned to see what Theodore meant and were rewarded with a splendid view of the young brachio relieving himself on the ornamental bushes at the hotel's entrance.

'NO!' Bea shouted, getting up. 'Budge, stop!' But it was too late: Budge was clearly settling in for an extended bathroom break, and there was nothing they could do to stop him. Bea could only hope that no one would notice, but sadly, that wasn't to be either. It is hard to avoid noticing an enormous brachiosaur, even if it isn't fully grown yet. The only brachiosaurs people usually saw were those chained up along the sides of roads or on beaches used as enormous living placards, their flanks painted with advertisements for SPAW or butcher's shops, as Budge had been. The remains of

Budge's body paint was now hidden under a layer of dirt from the road. Unfortunately, young and untrained as he was, he'd developed a habit of going whenever he wanted, regardless of who was around to see. In this case, it was the concierge, who came rushing out to shoo him away, flailing his arms and threatening to call the police.

Buster, coming to the aid of his new friend, bounded up the steps and knocked the man backwards with his huge muzzle. The concierge stumbled and shouted for help as Buster opened his mouth wide. Carter tutted his teeth loudly and instantly caught Buster's attention. He turned his yellow eyes to the boy. Carter shook his head and then stuck his tongue out at the Black Tyrant. Buster turned his attention back to the concierge, who was shaking in fear, and began licking him all over, leaving great trails of slobber all over his uniform. The concierge's cries, meanwhile, had attracted a number of bellboys and a desk clerk to come to his rescue, and when a fashionably attired guest ventured outside to see what all the fuss was about she emitted a series of high-pitched screams that sounded to Bea for all the world like a fire engine siren. Before Theodore could reassure her with the lie that Buster was an 'exotic allosaur', rather than a tyrant, and calm her down, she had fainted. Luckily, Theodore caught her before she hit the steps.

'OUT! OUT! OUT!' the concierge yelled, stabbing the air with his pointed hand at each of them in turn. His once perfectly slicked-back hair was a shambles, and now bore a large flap sticking straight up where Buster had swept his tongue along the side of his head. 'You are banned from the Hotel Espléndido!' he cried. 'Do not come back here ever again!'

'But my friend, the Viscount Knútr,' Theodore pleaded, 'I am to receive his messages here until he returns –'

'Take it up with the mayor!' the concierge retorted. 'None of you will set foot in my hotel!'

'Oh dear,' Bea said forlornly. By this time, Budge had finished his business, and looked about eagerly, ready to join in the fun it seemed all the humans were having. Instead, Bea led him away, and the others came close behind.

'On to Plan B,' Theodore announced when they were at a safe distance from the hotel. 'Or is it Plan C?'

Bea shot him a miserable look. 'Never mind,' Theodore countered. 'There's twenty-six letters in the alphabet – more than enough to go around.'

The delicious smells of foods wafted past as dinners were prepared in cafes and in the marketplace. Carter's belly rumbled. Bea dipped into her satchel and pulled out a paper bag.

'Sure you don't want any of my *chapulines?*' she offered, pouring some into her hand.

'No thanks.' Theodore shook his head. 'You're braver than me. I have a hard enough time looking at crickets, let alone after they have been fried and then gone soggy

wrapped in paper for a few days in the heat. You really should throw those away, Bea.'

'Not at all,' Bea retorted. 'I'm sure they're still delicious. Besides, it's my fault we're short on funds. I'll share mine with Budge here.'

The brachio turned away and eyed up a better option, a cart full of avocados. A man selling peanuts and tacos was setting up a stall nearby. Theodore motioned for Carter to lean closer, on the pretence of brushing a spider from his hair, but when he pulled his hand back, a coin glinted between his fingers. It was Carter's favourite trick.

'I thought you said we were out of money?' Carter asked, puzzled.

'Well, we are now,' Theodore replied. 'Go on,' he said kindly, 'get some for all of us.'

3

Arrival by Boat

~ *what's up, Buttercup?* ~

Yucatan Peninsula, Mexico, 1934

'Wake up, lazybones – we're here!'

Christian Hayter woke his Mountain Lythronax Tyrant with a bucket of cold dirty water.

Buttercup drowsily blinked open her eyes and turned to see the blurry form of her master standing in front of her.

The large container ship had docked and the regulations on importing live saurs were so strict that his tyrant had to be sedated and locked away in a container marked as SPAW. Hayter knew every trick in the book; smuggling goods and live exports past officials was one of his specialities. His dubious command over the black market trade in exotic Raptors of Paradise in Indonesia had come to an end, and now he was on the other side of the world smuggling a considerably larger tyrant past the beady eyes of government inspectors. The trick, as always,

was to distract them, and the presence of the army was the perfect decoy. The customs officials had completed their cursory sweep of the ship and were now inspecting the valuable cargo being unloaded onto the dock. The Doctor advised that it would take some time for Buttercup to come round from the powerful sedatives so he shut the door and went up to the deck to fetch another bucket of water. He scanned the dockside and noted that the army trucks, which were to transport their cargo, were all lined up, and soldiers milled around them taking a break. The chief customs official was now accompanied by a man in military uniform who was smoking a cigar.

A car horn sounded and a sleek long black car pulled up alongside them. When the driver opened the passenger door, out stepped the unmistakably sharp figure of Hayter's employer, the Viscount Von Lamprecht Knútr.

The man in uniform saluted then shook his hand as the last of the wooden crates were hauled down the gangplank by Hayter's most trusted men, Ash and Bishop. They were followed by the Doctor, dressed in his long black coat, black gloves, slicked-back hair and round dark glasses. The Viscount strolled onto the dock and gave Ash and Bishop a nod to crack one of the wooden crates open.

The official pulled a layer of straw aside to reveal the dull metal of weapons and munitions, all bearing the seal of the Sauria Firearms Corporation. Satisfied that the cargo was what was expected, the crate was resealed, and the men in uniform began loading them onto the trucks.

As the first pair approached the Doctor barked a stern warning. 'Be very careful! They've come a long way!' He motioned for them to slow down, then adjusted his dark glasses.

Seeing that everything was perfectly under control, and that the official would soon be gone, Hayter went back to douse Buttercup again. As the Mountain Lythronax stirred and got to her feet, Hayter gave her a little reminder who her boss was. All he had to do was raise his deadly clawed bullhook in the bright daylight so that the newly inlaid Saurman keystone could dazzle the saur. It certainly did the trick.

He smiled. 'What's up, Buttercup?'

The drugs had put her in a grouchy mood. Despite wanting to stretch her cramped muscles, she stood stock-still while Hayter tightened his saddle onto her back.

Suddenly the air outside was split by a burst of rapid gunfire coming from the dock. Hayter rushed to the deck to see that where before there was order, chaos now reigned. Masked men in shabby overalls were storming the dock, firing at the soldiers. Hayter froze as one of the men paused for a moment and looked his way. His mask was painted to look like a skull, so for a moment it seemed that death itself was staring at him. The man raised his rifle but Hayter ran back to his tyrant and leapt on. Buttercup stumbled unsteadily on her feet and slipped to the bottom of the gangway, almost toppling over the edge into the dirty bilge water.

He righted himself and spun round anxiously to see if Ash and Bishop had been hurt or worse. The bodies of wounded soldiers lay on the ground, and the trucks were taking off at speed. Pieces of

paper fluttered around in the air and were landing on the slain soldiers. The Viscount's car remained, but neither he nor the Doctor could be seen.

'What happened? Where are they?' Hayter shouted in a panic at the government official, who had regained his feet, and was clutching one of the many papers now floating through the air and around the dockside. On it was printed a skull and a slogan.

'It is the mark of the Rebels – th-they took them!' the man stuttered.

'What rebels? shouted Hayter, but the dazed man had become distracted by what he saw looming in front of him. It was clearly not a native tyrant, but an illegal import from North America. He tried to grab the reins and shouted for Hayter to dismount, but this was not to be his lucky day. Hayter swung his right foot and kicked him to the ground before rearing up and galloping off in the direction of the trucks.

✦ ✦ ✦

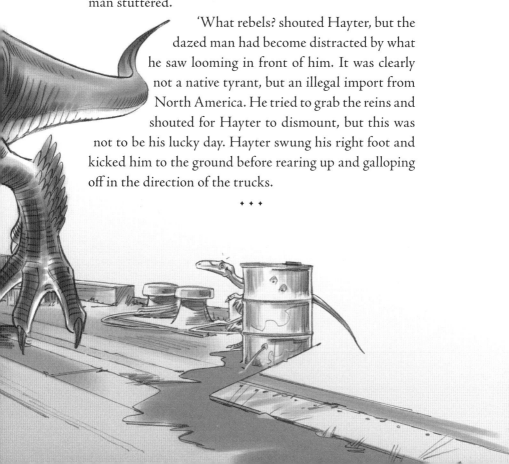

'Whoa there,' Hayter said softly to Buttercup as he came up to a fork in the road. He'd been riding for hours and it had got late. As the sun went down the jungle insects struck up their chatter, obscuring the sound of the trucks up ahead. A sign pointed towards a town, but the tracks seemed to have spun off in the other direction. Hayter followed them as best he could in the failing light until he spotted something glowing in the mud. He dismounted and went to see what it was – a cigar stub. He had to be near now. He got back up on Buttercup and urged her forward very slowly, until he could just make out the shapes of army vehicles in a clearing and hear merry voices congratulating one another. He made sure to remain hidden as he approached, the distant figures illuminated by the truck's headlights.

The Viscount and the Doctor were with a man dressed in shabby workmen's overalls holding a rifle and smoking a cigar. The three men were laughing.

Hayter knew he had to act quickly if he was to save them. He reached for his bullhook and let out a yell, charging into the clearing on his tyrant, scattering surprised Rebels as he did so.

'Why, Mr Hayter,' the Viscount announced, 'I was wondering when you'd catch up.'

'Quick, boss, jump on!' shouted Hayter as he turned quickly and knocked two of the Rebels over with the tyrant's tail.

The Viscount, however, remained rooted to the spot.

'What's going on?' Hayter demanded angrily, still wielding the bullhook above his head ready to swipe at anyone who got too close. 'Our cargo was for General Vulpez!'

The man smoking the cigar stepped forward. In his other hand he held a military-issue hat, which he slapped on his head. 'Welcome to Mexico, Mr Hayter,' he grinned. 'I'm General Vulpez.'

'What?'

'Come, Mr Hayter, rest your saur. That was a little performance on the dock to distract official eyes.'

'You shot and killed your own men?' Hayter spat.

'General Vulpez and I were just reflecting on how believable it was,' the Viscount said with a wide grin on his face.

'Don't worry, Mr Hayter,' the General drawled. 'My other soldiers are very much alive and well, and will return once the customs agent has taken his tale about a Rebel attack to town. It's amazing what you can do with blank bullets and salsa sauce.'

'Where are my men?' Hayter demanded.

'Safe over there,' the General offered, pointing to the last truck where they could be seen in the flicker of the Rebels' campfire.

'Why was I not told about this?' Hayter snapped. 'Why was I not taken with you?'

The General stepped up to the tyrant and marvelled at it. 'Quite a sight this is,' he explained. 'People don't ride tyrants in this country – we have titanosaurs here. They cause us a lot of trouble, and I don't think you could get a saddle on one if you tried.'

'There needed to be the element of surprise, Mr Hayter,' the Viscount said in a calm tone, 'and you were busy smuggling your saur and not where the action was. I was aware that the General had a plan but not what it was either until the moment it happened. The so-called Rebels are, in fact, the General's loyal guards. You'll catch on,' he added dismissively. 'Come, join us.'

Hayter finally dismounted and tethered Buttercup to a fence. 'General,' he barked, 'if your loyal guards don't get ample meat and water for Buttercup here, she'll pick them off one by one. She, like me, has quite a temper.'

The Doctor, meanwhile, was ordering people to carefully unload the crates from the trucks.

'Gently, gently,' he fussed, 'but be quick about it – the jungle cools down at night.'

The moonless night revealed that they were standing in a large clearing in the trees. The crates were being taken into a long, low wooden building in the middle of it.

'Since when were guns so delicate?' Hayter asked, genuinely puzzled. 'You've been watching over the crates like a hawk ever since we set sail.'

'Come,' the Doctor offered, and led them into the

building. It was lit by a series of bare lightbulbs that hung overhead, and was lined on both sides by long troughs of straw. 'Exactly as requested,' he said to the General with an appreciative nod. 'Start unloading,' the Doctor instructed Ash and Bishop. 'I'm sure the General is curious as to how the goods fared on the voyage.'

Hayter leant in as they prised open the first crate, tossed aside the straw, and removed a layer of rifles.

'Keep those safe,' the General ordered. 'I will need to return them to the authorities tomorrow . . . after I have recovered them from the Rebels!' As he laughed he bellowed smoke that the Doctor wafted away.

The next layer of straw was swept aside to reveal something wholly unexpected: a set of fifteen large eggs neatly nestled underneath.

The Doctor let out a sigh of relief and for a short moment smiled.

'Each one is the start of a whole new production line,' the Viscount explained, 'the most advanced of its kind in the world. The Viscount patted the Doctor on his shoulder.

'Inside these eggs are a new breed of Californian Longhorn Tritop that will grow bigger and mature more rapidly so that they can be sent to market at twice the usual speed.' He grinned as a group of men began carefully laying the eggs into the prepared troughs. 'In addition, their flesh is the best quality, and they are very docile, unlike the rubeosaurs native to this region. These tritops will not only one day soon feed the Revolution –' he nodded at General Vulpez, who nodded back – 'but the nation that the General will one day rule.'

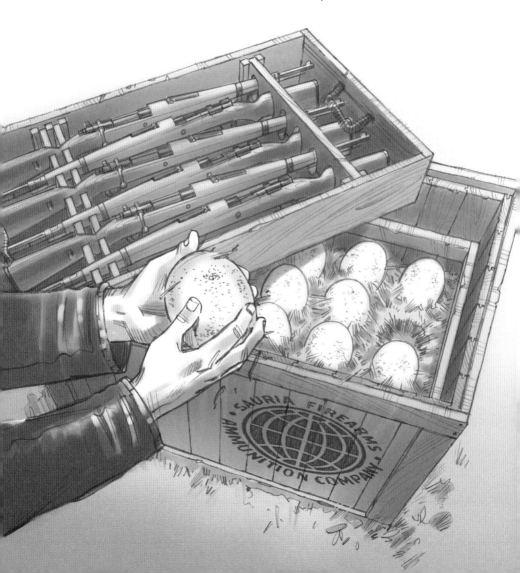

4

The Night Market

~ Sorry! ~

Bea, Carter and Theodore finished their impromptu dinner and set off to find alternative accommodation. It was clear that a town such as this wasn't built to allow saurs as large as Budge and Buster to roam the streets, as the buildings were close together and provided little room to pass. Only a few main avenues were broad, but these were lined with grand residences, municipal offices and a rather elaborate venue called *La Reina de Diamantes*, which Theodore told them must be a casino.

As they made their way through the market another obstacle presented itself: the attention of people astonished at the sight of a brachio being ridden by a girl, and a strange Black Tyrant upon which sat a boy and a man, whose attire clearly marked them as not being tourists. Nevertheless, they weren't locals, which made them targets for every kind of peddler trying to sell their wares. It was impossible to walk on for fear of trampling them. They were offered baskets and colourful woven rugs, clay pots and sombreros,

bead necklaces and pipes cut from hollow reeds. They were plied with ponchos and leather riding boots and felt slippers. People tried to sell them cactus salads and cones of *chapulines*, and chocolate and beer. Women thrust flowers up at them, and children offered newspapers and boxes of matches and packs of cigarettes. They waved off bananas and melons and decorated figurines and great big glazed and decorated breads.

'*Por favor*,' formed a chorus around them, '*por favor, por favor!*'

Annoyed at their refusals, one of the sellers yanked a big black feather from Buster's tail, causing him to spin round to confront his tormenter. In doing so, he nearly toppled Theodore and Carter from their saddle and overturned a cart, sending ripe avocados tumbling into the street, some of which became instant guacamole under Buster's giant feet. A woman selling parasols took the opportunity to poke Budge away from her stall to avoid upsetting her wares, but it had the opposite effect, as he swept his head round, knocking several opened ones to the ground and many more rolling down the street like a cascade of painted logs.

Suddenly the crowd, which moments before had been imploring them to stop and sample their goods, turned hostile, and shouted at them to be gone. But where could they go? As soon as they moved in one direction people appeared and the way grew narrow – but turning caused more havoc than before. Budge, who didn't like small spaces, panicked and stumbled off, knocking over tables and crushing displays as he went, picking up speed. Carter and Theodore had no choice but to follow in the path he created. 'Sorry! Sorry!' they cried as they leapt along, truly mortified at the destruction they caused. Almost at the market's edge Budge ran through a balloon-seller's stall, pulling a dozen by their long strings, still attached to the bricks that prevented them from flying away. Too late now, Budge bounded ahead with them swirled about his neck like a scarf, as one by one they came undone and escaped into the night sky.

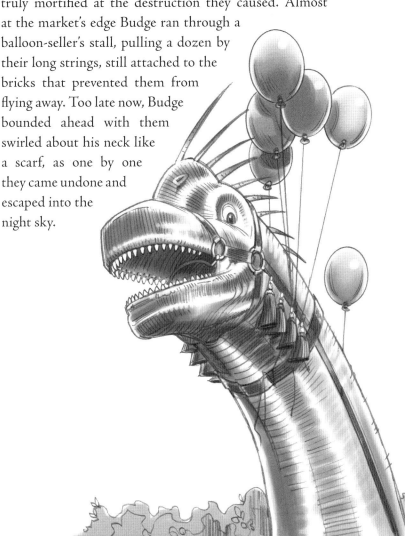

Behind them, a crowd of angry locals waved their fists and shouted insults at their backs. 'Basta!' they cried over and over again. 'Enough! Enough!'

Someone angrily swatted Budge's flank with a straw broom, just missing Bea's leg, causing him to flinch and whine. 'Hey!' Bea cried, whirling round to face their attacker, only to find that others were reaching for sticks and brandishing them menacingly all around her. Someone else tossed pieces of shattered watermelon at them, and Carter cried out when he and Buster were doused with a bucketful of dirty water.

Eager to get away, they stomped out of the market and raced as fast as they could towards the edge of town. As they flew Carter's heart thumped in his ears and tears streamed down Bea's cheeks unchecked.

Soon enough the lights of Mérida were just a glow on the horizon and the evening air sparkled instead with fireflies and glow-worms that mesmerised Buster, who tried to catch them with his tongue. The stone buildings had given way to adobe houses, which then thinned out to wooden shacks as the town merged with the jungle. Small patches of cleared land used to grow crops were interspersed with warehouses. The sounds of human activity were gradually replaced by the din of insects as the vegetation increased.

It was Carter who finally broke the heavy silence which hung over them like a cloud. 'What's Plan C?' he asked with more optimism in his voice than he really felt.

Theodore turned to see Bea holding onto the brachiosaur's neck as he swung round and into a leafy tree.

'Well, we can't go back.' Theodore nodded towards a glow increasing in size further up the road. 'Looks like the next village is not too far – let's hope we have better luck there.'

Bea, Carter and Theodore walked on in silence and soon found themselves on the outskirts of a small village that clung to the edge of the jungle, where the air grew heavy and fragrant. The sound of music and people laughing grew stronger until they emerged from some houses into a square all strung with lights. Tables were set up at one end, and a Mariachi band was playing on a small stage. People of all ages were dancing and making merry. No one had noticed them approach.

Bea nudged Carter and pointed to two people who appeared to be the centre of attention. 'It's a wedding,' she remarked.

'Hold on,' Theodore said in a hushed voice, holding out his arm to halt them. 'We don't want to ruin this occasion.' Theodore looked behind him. 'Five minutes back there was a pond. Let's rest Budge and let Buster have a dip safely out of the way.'

5

Poppo Miguel and the Canteras

~ part of the family ~

Having safely left the exhausted Buster and Budge to satisfy themselves splashing in the nearby pond, Bea, Carter and Theodore returned to the square. The smell of food was impossible to ignore and made their stomachs rumble. The wedding feast was laid out tantalisingly in front of them, and the *chapulines* from before had done nothing for their hunger. They sat themselves down at a table and considered what to do next.

'How much money do we have left, Bea?' Carter asked.

Bea rummaged in her satchel. 'Not enough,' she said.

'Not enough for what?' Carter asked.

'Anything,' Bea confirmed. She looked downcast.

'It's not your fault,' Theodore said.

'Yes it is,' she replied. 'You tried your best to stop me, but I had to have him. I forgot we were using pesos, and lost track of how much the price was going up.'

'Your grandmother once bid on a "masterpiece"

painted by an elephant at a charity auction,' Theodore said, consoling her. 'It was allegedly a very good likeness of an orangutan who lived in the same zoo. Zebedee, his name was.'

Carter giggled.

'Thankfully someone else walked off with the prize, but it was close. I suppose Bunty did the right thing by driving the price up. Dreadfully fine-looking chap, Zebedee. That elephant really captured how orange he was about the face.'

Bea punched him playfully in the ribs. 'Stop it!' she cried. 'You're not making me feel any better – your story is funny, but mine isn't. What are we going to do?'

'You did the right thing, Bea,' Carter said. 'You saved Budge from being sold to someone who would hurt him badly. Now he has people who care for him.'

'But we're here to look for the Twins' lost city,' Bea said, 'not rescue every saur we come across just because we feel like it. Lambert gave us that money to finance this trip, not to add to the number of mouths we have to feed.'

'What's done is done,' Theodore said firmly. 'No more talk of regrets. Let's rest here a while and figure things out in the morning. These people seem friendly.'

'Bea,' Carter said, and nudged his sister. 'That boy keeps staring at you.'

Bea looked up to see a handsome boy, about as old as she was, smiling at her from the crowd. As soon as he

caught her eye he walked over and held out his hand. Bea hesitated, then grinned and stood up.

'Javier,' the boy said by means of introduction.

'Beatrice,' Bea replied, 'but everyone calls me Bea.' He motioned for her to follow, and Theodore nodded, so off they went and melted into the happy throng.

It wasn't long before Carter, too, was led away by a conga line that passed close to the table. Theodore relaxed and watched as Carter became the centre of attention when he cheekily swiped a woman's scarf and proceeded to re-create his shadow raptor dance to the delight of the crowd.

Meanwhile, an elderly man, who appeared to be blind, slowly sidled up to the table, felt for a seat, and plopped onto it. It was uncertain if he was aware that someone was already sitting at the table until he called for two drinks to be brought over, and motioned one to be given to Theodore.

'Cheers!' Theodore said, and the old man raised his bottle, too.

'Even I can't dance as long as I used to,' the elderly man said with a smile, 'but you're still young.'

'How can you tell?' Theodore asked, but the man just grinned.

A voice from behind him said, 'Excuse the old man, he's blind and clumsy but still can't resist dancing with the ladies.' It was the woman from whom Carter had 'borrowed' a scarf.

'Sorry about the . . .' Theodore began, tipping his head towards the dancing.

'That's okay,' the woman said. 'I'm Lucia Cantera – and that's Poppo.'

'Logan, Theodore Logan,' he offered, 'pleased to meet you both.'

'It seems our children are having more fun than we are – come, let's dance,' she offered.

'Oh, I don't dance,' Theodore demurred, 'and they're not really my children.'

'Nonsense,' Lucia said with a smile. 'Everyone dances in Mexico!'

Theodore shrugged. 'I'm not dressed for it.'

'No, you look good,' said Lucia, getting up and holding out her hand. 'Besides, no one should be better dressed than the groom!'

It was impossible to refuse such an invitation. If an ancient blind man could dance, well, Theo thought, he should be able to as well.

'So whose children are they if not yours?' Lucia asked, as they twirled to the music.

'It's a long story,' Theodore replied. 'Who's Poppo?'

'Poppo Miguel is my father-in-law,' Lucia answered.

Theodore's grip loosened momentarily. 'You're married?' he asked, glancing around to see if there were a thousand eyes on his back.

'My husband is dead,' Lucia told him. 'Poppo and my son, Javier, are all the family I have.'

'I'm sorry to hear that,' Theodore said, relief in his voice. He changed the subject quickly. '*Poppo* – that means grandfather, right?' he asked.

'Yes,' Lucia replied, 'though he's really everyone's grandfather. Even the old people call him Poppo. That man is made of different stuff. He's outlived all his friends.' She swirled around and continued. 'He still acts like a young man, but trapped in an old man's body.'

They looked on as Poppo Miguel, who'd made his way back to the centre of the square, laughed and swirled around in time with the music, his hands placed gently

about the hips of a young lady, who was following his every move.

'I know how he feels,' Theodore commented under his breath.

'We don't get many strangers around here,' Lucia said. 'Where are you travelling from?'

'We were going to stay in town at the Hotel Espléndido,' Theodore replied carefully, 'but I decided we should experience some local flavour instead – you know, see the real Mexico, rather than the places you see in brochures.'

Lucia didn't look convinced. 'Tourists don't usually travel with saurs,' she pointed out. 'I saw you leading them to the pond when you arrived.'

'Ah yes,' Theodore acknowledged, 'but Buster and Budge are part of the family. Where we go, they go.'

6

The Last Brachio Herder

~ a city lost in the jungle ~

Bea was jolted awake by a tap on her shoulder. She'd been dreaming she was still at sea on the Orca, rocking gently in Captain Woods' hammock, re-reading her father's journal. She opened her eyes expecting to see the cabin, but all she saw were leaves.

'Careful,' a voice warned as she went to sit up. 'It's a long way down!'

She was in a string hammock nestled between two wide branches of a tree overhanging the pond in which Buster and Budge had bathed earlier. She paused, then reached for the leather satchel she'd been resting her head on, to make sure the strap was still slung round her shoulders. Sure enough, it was there. She then patted her chest to find her locket and the keystone in place, as she did every time she woke.

'Good morning – what's left of it!' the voice said, and she gingerly turned her head to see where it was coming from. Down below on the ground she made out the black-feathered bulk of Buster, with Carter snuggled up to him, and, close by, Theodore slumped against Budge, who bore a

few deflated balloons about his tail. It all came back to her: this was where they'd ended up last night after the wedding in the square. Then a nutshell hit her on the head. When she looked up she saw a pair of brown eyes peeking from a branch higher up.

'Welcome to my tree,' Javier said, and shrugged. 'Sorry – I'm not usually that good a shot!'

✦ ✦ ✦

Once they'd climbed down, Bea and Javier left the saurs and the others sleeping and headed in the direction of Javier's house, a small but comfortable looking cottage on the edge of the village closest to the pond.

'What's your punk's name?' Javier asked as they walked.

'Sorry?' Bea was confused. 'What punk?'

'Young brachiosaurs are called punks, you know,' Javier replied.

'Oh! His name's Budge,' Bea told him. 'Because sometimes he doesn't budge when you want him to.'

'He's a handsome beast,' Javier said hesitantly. 'You don't often see a tame brachio around here. Where did you get him?'

'I won him,' Bea quickly lied. 'At a rodeo. In San Diego. Doing trick-riding. First place. Loads of competition. I used to do trick-riding with my cousins.'

'Really?' Javier responded. 'You got a brachio not a trophy?'

'Yes – just this guy,' Bea said, glancing at Javier. 'He's

far better than some trophy any day.' She didn't feel ready to disclose the whole story of how she came to own a brachiosaur who seemed to cause trouble wherever he went. Despite her good intentions, and Carter's reassurance that she'd done the right thing, she still felt it didn't reflect well upon her. She'd been so careless spending all of their money on him. She recalled the moment the auctioneer's agent presented them with the bill and she felt her stomach drop once more, just like it had then. She'd tried to explain to the auctioneer that she hadn't understood how the price had shot up in pesos, but the man hurried her along. He had no patience for a stupid little girl, and as far as he was concerned she'd bought herself a nice new pet. Theodore had counted out the money without saying a word of reproach, which had made her feel even worse. She wished he'd simply tell her off and be done with it, the way Bunty would have done.

'Well, you have your work cut out for you,' Javier said. 'Brachios aren't easily tamed. They prefer to be free.'

'I'm beginning to see that,' Bea replied pensively, and yawned.

♦ ♦ ♦

Theodore cupped the steaming mug of coffee between his hands carefully. As they sat round the table in the courtyard of the Canteras' modest home, Theodore tried to compose an answer to Lucia's question that didn't sound utterly ridiculous. He wasn't succeeding.

'Why are we here? We're here to . . . to . . .'

Carter, who didn't understand Theodore's hesitancy amongst such obvious friends, cut in with the truth. 'We're looking for the lost city,' he explained in a gush.

'*Everyone* has heard of the lost city,' Javier said.

Theodore went to kick Carter under the table, but hit Bea's leg instead.

'What he means to say is that we're here waiting for a lost friend of ours *in the city*,' Bea clarified. 'Lambert – he's a viscount.' As soon as she said it she kicked herself. She'd wanted to impress Javier, but he didn't look impressed.

'He's in Mexico on business and he's staying at the Hotel Espléndido,' Theodore added.

'No he's not,' Carter chimed in.

'I see,' said Lucia knowingly. It was clear their guests needed to get their story straight.

Theodore coughed to catch Carter's attention but it was no use.

'And the hotel man kicked us out after Buster licked him,' Carter added, and before anyone could stop him he added, 'and Budge going to the toilet on his flower beds. Then we accidentally broke everything in the market when we were running away.' He pointedly ignored Theodore's desperate glaring. 'And we lost all our money,' he tacked on as an afterthought.

Poppo Miguel laughed. 'You made an enemy of the hotel manager?' he asked. 'Then you are not alone, my friends. He's only popular amongst . . . a certain class of people. I have known him since he was a boy. He only likes wealthy people and he cheats at cards.'

'So why are you really here?' Lucia tried again.

Theodore sighed. 'It's a long story. I know it sounds crazy, but we are here to look for a city lost in the jungle, and our friend Lambert was supposed to help us. He was going to put us up at the hotel, but he's gone.'

'You're looking for a needle in a haystack,' Lucia offered, delivering a fresh batch of churros to the table. 'Many people have looked for this fabled city, and all have failed.'

At this Poppo Miguel huffed.

'Poppo worked his whole life in the jungle,' Lucia continued. 'Did you ever see a city there?'

The old man shook his head. 'It's best lost for ever.'

'What was your job?' Bea asked, biting into a warm and crispy churro. The sweet pastry was delicious.

'My grandfather and my father were both Brachio Herders,' explained Javier.

'A Brachio Herder is someone given the lifelong task of living with and protecting the wild brachios from entering and flattening the villages close to the jungle,' Lucia explained. 'The brachios and people lived safely apart for many years. That was until people started to cut down the jungle bit by bit to graze cattle and grow crops. Then business found ways to make money from the jungle, turning it into plantations and farmland, and it's being cut down at an alarming rate. With no Brachio Herders to control them, the wild brachios trampled the fences and valuable livestock escaped.'

'Oh, I understand – a Herder is someone who looks after saurs!' Bea exclaimed and nodded to Theodore. 'So the brachios just wanted their land back.'

'Yes,' replied Lucia. 'Thankfully the president understands the problem, and has halted all large-scale farming in order to preserve the landscape and the brachiosaurs' environment.'

'Sounds like a wise leader,' Theodore commented. 'But surely the corporations haven't taken this lying down?'

'You're right,' Lucia said. 'But there is a new problem. No one dares go into the jungle any more because the Rebels set up camps there. It's dangerous.'

'Yes – we encountered them coming into town,' Bea remarked.

'And the Rebels are being supported by these corporations, I suppose,' Theodore said.

Lucia sighed. 'People go where the money is. It's just human nature.'

'Mama used to work for the avocado plantation,' said Javier, 'and that's in the jungle. That's how she knows about the Rebels.'

'*Basta*, Javier,' Lucia cut in.

'But she left and we too are short of money now,'

Javier continued.

'I told you not talk of the plantation,' Lucia said in a stern voice.

'But –' Javier protested.

'Not to anyone, Javier,' she said in a low voice. 'Even friends.'

Bea and Theodore looked at each other. Clearly they weren't the only ones with secrets to hide.

'A brachio was killed,' Poppo Miguel interjected, and shook his head.

'Poppo!' Lucia cried, shooting him a glance that he could not see. 'That goes for you, too!' At that, she got up abruptly and went inside.

They all turned to look at Poppo Miguel and waited for him to elaborate, but he didn't say anything else. He just sipped at his coffee and took a bite of his churro.

✦ ✦ ✦

Carter and Javier carried a couple of buckets of fish parts out to Buster, while Bea made sure Budge hadn't eaten all of the leaves on Javier's tree. Carter had some questions of his own.

'Why is Poppo Miguel blind?' he asked.

Javier shrugged. 'He's very old. His eyesight started failing before he came to live with us after my father died.'

'My father died too, and my mother,' Carter said. 'They were killed by shadow raptors,' he said in a low voice. 'How about yours?'

'Stampede,' Javier replied. 'He was guiding some wild brachios away from a village when someone started shooting at them. It caused a stampede. My father's beloved brachio was fatally wounded and fell, crushing him.'

'Was he a Brachio Herder too?'

'Yes, but now Poppo Miguel is the last of his kind.'

'Sorry to hear that,' Carter replied, and offered his new friend a sympathetic smile.

'Poppo wanted me to follow the family tradition to be a Brachio Herder,' Javier said, shrugging his shoulders, 'but it's over – that way of life ended with my father.'

'You don't want to be a Brachio Herder?' Carter asked.

'I don't want to die like one,' Javier replied gravely, and paused. 'There are not many good jobs around here; only

the plantation pays well. No one wants
to herd brachios for a living.'

'Why didn't your mother want to
talk about the plantation?'
Carter quizzed.

'My mother is a strong
woman with a big heart,' Javier
replied. 'She wants nothing
to do with it any more.'

7

The Welcome Guests

~ *Plan D* ~

'Thank you so much for your wonderful hospitality,' Theodore told Lucia as he helped clean up from breakfast, 'but we must be going.'

Bea, overhearing this, objected loudly and pulled Theodore aside. For the first time since leaving her cousins, May and Violet, back in America, she had felt the joy of companionship, and she was reluctant to quit so soon. Carter and Theodore couldn't make up for friends of her own age, and she was enjoying getting to know Javier. 'Can't we stay a little while longer, at least until Lambert returns?' she asked.

'I think it's quite an imposition for us to stay,' said Theodore apologetically, 'and we don't know when he'll return. Perhaps it's best if we went with Plan D.'

'Plan D?' Bea demanded, exasperated. 'I suppose Plan D involves selling Budge to fund the rest of our trip.'

'It might not come to that,' Theodore said gently. 'Not yet. But it's a possibility you might have to consider, Bea.'

'We don't have to wait for Lambert,' Bea urged. 'We

can ask around – show Javier the map, or Lucia – see if anyone can understand it. We've come so far! The lost city must be around here somewhere – Lambert said so! Why can't we just head into the jungle to take a look?'

'I'm sorry, Bea,' Theodore said. 'You heard what Lucia said – the jungle is a dangerous place to be.'

He was interrupted by Javier, who'd come back from fishing in the pond with Carter. 'What map?' Javier asked.

Bea and Theodore exchanged a look of caution before Bea decided that her friendship might depend on tossing that to the wind. 'My father was an explorer – Franklin Kingsley. He and my mother Grace went all over the world looking for . . . temples before they were killed,' she explained. 'In his journals he left notes about the people who once lived in an ancient city here in Mexico. It must be what is now known as the lost city.'

'Mérida is the biggest town around here,' Javier scoffed. 'And it's no city!'

'Apparently the Saurmen lived there,' added Bea. 'Have you heard of them?'

'Bea,' Theodore warned.

A voice came from the corner of the room. It was Poppo Miguel. 'What else do these notes say?'

Bea jumped at the chance to share. She withdrew from her satchel her father's journal that Lambert had given her and opened it where some pages had clearly been torn out. She was about to point to them, but realised that Poppo

Miguel wouldn't be able to see. Lucia and Javier crowded round as Theodore rolled his eyes to the sky in despair.

'This is where he starts talking about a source of keystones and the birth place of the twins,' Bea explained.

'Twins?' Lucia remarked. 'Is he referring to the Gemini Festival that happens in a few weeks?'

'Sorry, I don't understand,' said Bea. 'The next pages are missing. After that, he writes about the Mayans and human sacrifice – it's a bit gory.'

'Now that bit's true,' Javier confirmed. 'We learnt all about that in school.' He shuddered at the thought.

'I wanted to know what might have been on those missing pages,' Bea continued. 'And one day, while I was with my cousins, we were doing rubbings of different types of bark around their ranch.' She stopped. 'Do you know what that is?' she asked Javier.

'Yes, it's where you make a copy of something by making a print of it on paper by rubbing crayon or chalk.'

'Right!' said Bea. 'Well, it gave me an idea. I did the same thing to the page after the torn-out bits, and sure enough, my father's pencil had left an impression.' She pulled out a thin piece of paper with the rubbing on it from the front of the book and held it up. 'I didn't need the missing page to know what had been on it. At first I thought it was a doodle or a pattern like the ones my mother practised in her sketchbook, but then I realised it was a map!'

'Of this place?' Javier asked.

'It appears so, yes,' Bea confirmed.

Javier looked closer. 'I don't recognise the circles,' he said.

'Not sure what they are,' Bea said. 'At first I thought it was a place where he was getting the ink in his pen to work, and that the letters "CHICXULUB" were nonsense until I found it in the index of my cousin's atlas when we were playing a game where you have to find places that have animal names. I was given "Chicken". Sure enough, it looked like a rough outline of the Yucatan Peninsula. Our journey was financed by a good friend of ours, Lambert, who knew our parents. He too has an interest in the Saurmen. Once we told him about our discovery, he jumped right on board, and insisted we try to find it.'

'He's my godfather,' Carter spoke up proudly.

Bea handed Javier the rubbing and he held it up to the light.

'Yes – it does looks like a map of here,' he said, running his finger along a few recognisable contours, 'but half is missing.'

Bea nodded. 'That must have been on the left-hand page but we only have an impression of the right-hand page.'

Lucia shook her head. 'That could be anywhere,' she pointed out, laughing. 'You have come all this way with half a map and a bunch of jumbled-up stories!'

'It must around here somewhere,' Bea said. 'Father was never wrong. All we need to do is figure out what part of the jungle it's in. Theo can lead us to it after that. He has a knack of being able to find things which are supposed to be hidden.'

'Is that so?' Poppo Miguel said. 'How interesting. What have you found so far?'

'He found the saur graveyard back in California,' Bea said. 'Didn't you, Theo?'

It was too late now to go back. 'Indeed I did,' Theodore admitted.

'And the twins,' Carter added for good measure. He'd been most impressed with them when Theodore had taken them back for a closer look.

'And the twins,' Theodore agreed.

Poppo Miguel's face remained impassive.

'Then you should stick around.' Lucia smiled. 'At the Gemini Festival you will find lots of people and saurs dressing up as twins. But I warn you, you must not go into the jungle,' Lucia insisted. 'I tell you, you will regret it.' She turned to face Theodore. 'I'll tell you because I think you should know. I worked for the new avocado plantation just inside the trees over here. We had to help clear away the wood, and from what I could see they must have been using brachios to help them somehow,' she said. 'There was a lot of brachio dung about – too much. The owners said they would pay very well, so I did not ask too many questions, but I knew something was not right with the place. Then one day we heard a terrible noise – a titanosaur must have been attacking a brachiosaur close by. People were screaming for help and some of my friends ran over to the next clearing to see what was going on.' She paused. 'They never came back.'

Bea brought her hands to her mouth in shock. 'Oh my!'

'I finished my shift and told them I needed paying as I was not coming back. A man got very angry with me, and said I would not get paid for any of the work unless I finished my contract, but they owed me over three months' pay. They told me that if I came back and told no one what I saw and heard, I would get paid more. But I decided not to go back. What I saw would have broken my husband's heart if he were still alive. I left without my wages.'

'Should you not tell the authorities about this?' asked Bea naively.

Lucia shook her head. 'People around here depend on avocado farming,' she explained. 'I can't go causing them trouble, but these people are not to be trusted.' She shrugged and folded her arms. 'So now I have told you my secret,' she said. 'Theodore, it's time to tell us yours!'

Bea noted Lucia's stance and also crossed her arms in support. Theodore needed to trust people more; she was always telling him that.

'He's not ready,' Poppo Miguel said to the surprise of all. Theodore looked relieved. The Stegosorcerer had warned him not to reveal that he was a Saurman too readily, as he would need to take some time to process it and try to figure out his place in this strange new world of which he was a part.

'Mama.' Javier spoke up. 'In less than two weeks it will be the Gemini Festival. Why can't they stay a while, and wait until their friend arrives? We can use the time to try to figure out what could be on the other half of the map.'

Lucia nodded at her son and smiled at her guests. 'I doubt you will find out what's on the map – the jungle grows thick and fast, so who knows what has changed since that map was drawn. But please, do stay. We would all be glad to have you – and Budge and Buster!'

Carter immediately held out his hand to shake on it. 'Deal!' he announced gleefully.

8

The Brachio Circle

~ an audacious operation ~

The loud chirruping of insects was an effective alarm clock. Hayter rose and made his way out of the tent. The familiar sound of snoring from another tent told him that Ash and Bishop were still asleep. It had been hard to make out in the dark, but he found himself standing in a large clearing that was almost perfectly circular. The buildings housing the tritop hatchery sat in the middle. They had been constructed from the timber that had grown there. Indeed, where a majestic jungle had once stood since the dawn of time, now flat, manicured grass formed a circular lawn. Workers were busy building wooden pens from some of the ammunition crates for the imminent hatching of tritop eggs, bustling in and out of the hatcheries like bees at a hive. Three men stood in the clearing – the Viscount, the Doctor and General Vulpez. Hayter made his way over to them.

'The hatchery is exactly as I specified,' the Doctor was saying, 'but the people here need training if they are to rear the tritops efficiently.'

The Viscount turned to the General. 'We will need to hire more of these local farmers. Doctor Achtecka here will stay on and see that it is done properly.'

The General rubbed his stubbly square chin. 'That can be arranged, but it will cost more. If you increase payments and keep your part of the deal, it can be done,' he replied and grinned.

'Ah, Mr Hayter has decided to join us,' the Doctor mused. 'I hope you had pleasant dreams. You are well rested, I trust?'

'What's with the circle?' Hayter asked gruffly, sweeping his arm to indicate the clearing's perimeter. 'That must have taken an enormous amount of manpower. The jungle's thick around here.'

The General chuckled. 'You're just in time for my morning tour. Come, let me show you,' he said, and beckoned them all to follow. As they walked over to another clearing, he explained the set-up. 'Most of the men and women working here are ordinary farmers who have been hired to grow and farm avocados – at least, that's what they think they're doing,' he said and winked. 'But really it's our cover story for this new venture in farming Californian Longhorn Tritops.'

'Does the president still think that turning the jungle into farmland is a bad idea? When I last met him he was very much against it,' the Viscount remarked.

'Don't you worry, señor,' the General said. 'In time, the president will come to see my way of thinking . . . or be replaced.' He adjusted his top button and set his oversized hat straight. 'I will make a new policy allowing us to legally clear the jungle to farm tritops, but for now we're setting everything up so we can establish this new "crop", and fear of the Rebels keeps prying eyes away.'

'But tell me, General Vulpez,' Hayter asked, 'won't

these farmers realise pretty quickly they're not growing avocados? How can we trust all these locals to turn a blind eye and not tell anyone?'

The General laughed and lit another cigar. 'These people only know about their own small part in this big operation. None of them get to see the whole picture. I use one set of people to help clear the jungle, and when they finish that job, I move them onto a new site. Then a different set of people remove the valuable wood, and then carpenters build the fences and huts. They all think we are setting up an avocado plantation. By the time they notice that no avocados are being grown it will be too late. Besides, they will have been paid and moved on. They will have no cause for complaint.' He swept his hand about. 'These people you see around you are my most trusted associates, and they will care for the tritops for now.'

'But the locals go home to families and friends,' the Doctor pointed out. 'Surely they will discuss what they see here.'

'Señor Viscount's money buys their silence, and I make sure they understand what happens if they talk. I have a way of making people do what I want. Take my loyal guards for instance. They will do anything I ask of them.'

'You must be working these farmers day and night to clear the jungle,' Hayter remarked. 'How are they doing it?'

His question was answered when they entered another circular clearing that was identical in scope to the first, but

at an earlier stage of development.

'This is how we have solved our hard-labour issue,' General Vulpez grinned as they broke through the undergrowth.

Near the circle's edge was a massive wild Yucatan Brachiosaur nibbling away at the canopy of green at the edge of the clearing. Its back foot was tethered by a giant chain, which was locked to a metal pike embedded in the centre of the cleared circle.

'It only takes a couple of weeks for a single brachiosaur to create the grazing land we need for our operation,' he explained. 'We let the chain out a little at a time to expand the area. And of course –' he coughed – 'they fertilise as they go.'

Everyone gazed up at the huge saur, at its impressive bulk, and its belly swollen from gorging on the lush vegetation.

'Wonderful!' The Viscount clapped his hands together. 'I love the simplicity of this operation, and the sheer scale of it is so audacious!'

'What about the remaining trees?' Hayter asked, pointing to bare stumps stripped of everything green. 'Surely they don't eat those too?'

'It's true – they don't like being tethered, and often become enraged,' said the General. 'They are quite willing

to knock those down in a fit of anger, especially when they come to the end of the chain and can no longer reach the leaves.' He shot Hayter a sly smile. 'We now deliberately let them go hungry so that they knock them all down.'

Hayter took a swig of water from his hip flask. 'Clever,' he agreed.

'We sell off most of the quality timber and use the rest to build the fences and pens. After this brachio has done his part then we'll move a herd of armargas in.' The General pointed to the next circular clearing where the strange saurs' long neck spines could be seen silhouetted in the morning light. 'They are more docile and quite useful for keeping the weeds down. The jungle always wants to grow back, so we let them munch this down to the ground and fertilise it some more. Only then do we sow grass for the tritops to eat.'

'Free labour,' Hayter remarked, 'and maximum profit.' He sounded grudgingly impressed.

'But watch out for these wild brachios,' the General warned. 'Especially with your tyrant. They may be chained, but if you get too close they will defend their territory fiercely. One kick or swipe of that tail can kill you instantly,' he snapped, clicking his fingers. 'Even titanosaurs have a hard time bringing one down, but they like to try. We are having more and more trouble with them. One was taken down last week – a rather unfortunate incident when a few of the farmers were crushed.'

'Titanosaurs, you say?' The Doctor's blank expression momentarily lit up as he and the Viscount caught each other's eyes.

'I can imagine you have trouble with a free meal tied to a chain,' the Viscount quipped.

'Exactly, señor, and that is why we're now a little behind our clearance schedule. Our success depends on keeping our machines –' he pointed to the brachio – 'from being eaten while they work.'

'I am impressed with everything, General Vulpez,' the Viscount concluded, 'but we can't let production fall behind at any cost. We will soon have hundreds of tritop hatchlings to feed.' He paused before continuing. 'However, I may have a solution to our troubles,' he said, and glanced at Hayter and the Doctor, who was swatting a mosquito on his arm with his black gloves.

'Go on,' the General said.

'Well, I would most certainly like to claim a wild titanosaur's head for my trophy wall back home.' The Viscount smiled. 'I have quite an expansive collection, you know.'

'And I would like to see inside one, if we have time, Herr Viscount,' the Doctor added.

'Trapping one here and disposing of it will just encourage more to come back when they smell blood,' warned General Vulpez.

'Are there any other saurs around here in the jungle?

Carnivores we could use that might be able to keep guard?' Hayter asked.

'There are plenty of Irritators about,' the General replied, 'but they are a lot less fierce than they look. They're actually quite stupid creatures and run away at the first hint of trouble. They eat rodents, my friends, not titanosaurs.'

'Irritators,' Hayter said thoughtfully. 'They're like the Baryonyx we have back in England. I've seen them put up a good fight when need be.' He tapped the bullhook that hung from his belt. 'They can be trained. Anything else with teeth and claws?'

'Plenty,' the General answered, 'but they are all smaller and not good for anything.'

'Give me a couple of days for my men to round up some of these Irritators and see if we can teach them some tricks,' Hayter retorted, and he grinned at the Doctor, who glanced back at him through his darkened glasses.

'Any help would be gratefully received, Mr Hayter,' General Vulpez said, 'but I really can't see Irritators being of any use in our enterprise.'

'Do not be so quick to write off Mr Hayter's abilities with saurs, General Vulpez,' the Viscount murmured to Hayter's surprise. 'He has a way of making the most mild-mannered things quite angry.' The Viscount fixed a gaze on the General that made it clear he was not joking. 'And Doctor Achtecka here will oversee the training of the new farmers and collect some specimens for his research. If you don't mind, I would like to return after I have concluded some personal business in town and shoot a titanosaur for my collection. See to it that one is lured and trapped here for me to make the kill, would you, Mr Hayter?'

Hayter nodded.

'Good,' the General remarked, 'then I will return in a few days. Now, if you will excuse me – when I'm not plotting against the president, I'm pretending to protect him. I have a victory over the Rebels to stage, involving the triumphant return of these fine weapons. Apparently those naughty boys caused quite a scene at the docks yesterday. The president looks very kindly upon those who quash the Rebels.' He brushed some dust from the shining array of medals attached to his chest. 'I might have to award myself another one of these for bravery,' he muttered, and extinguished his cigar on the floor. 'Until next time,' he said suavely, and left.

'Can he be trusted?' Hayter asked as they watched the General's vehicle drive off, kicking up a cloud of dust.

'I very much hope so,' the Viscount remarked. 'I've invested a great deal of money in this venture so far, and his loyalty doesn't come cheap.'

9

A Fool's Errand

~ a token of appreciation ~

The next morning, Javier introduced Carter and
Bea to his friends, who were all curious to meet
the new arrivals in the village and the saurs
that travelled with them. Despite punk brachios having
a playful disposition, everyone knew that they were still
quite a danger to be around. A tame one, therefore, was
a rarity, even in these parts. Tyrants of any kind were to
be avoided, so to also have a passive exotic Black Dwarf to
look at up close and feed fish heads was a real treat.

'People are very cautious of large carnivores around
here,' Javier said, tossing another fish head into the air for
Buster to snatch and swallow with glee. He'd been a bit
nervous around him and Budge at first, but soon warmed
up after seeing how comfortable Bea and Carter were
around the large saurs. Carter showed him how to gain his
trust and pet his feathers properly to help him overcome
his fear.

'I noticed there aren't many allosaurs about?'
Bea enquired.

'Allos are not as popular as in North America,' Javier replied, 'because as meat-eaters they cost a lot to feed. It's easier to keep and feed mimusaurs.'

'Do you have any tyrants here in Mexico?' asked Carter.

Javier shook his head. 'Some further south towards the mountains. Here we have titanosaurs.' He held out three fingers on both hands and mocked an attack. 'You don't want to meet a titanosaur, who is twice the size of Buster here, with bigger arms and three clawed fingers.'

Carter raised his eyes in wonder. 'Buster is a Dwarf Tyrant,' he said proudly. 'He is fully grown but looks fatter than he is because of all his feathers.'

'I've only seen tyrants in books,' Javier replied, 'partially covered in feathers, and never all black.'

'They help him float in water like a duck,' Carter explained. 'Here,' he said, lifting one of Buster's forelimbs. 'Feel this – it's a pocket of loose skin between his arm and body.' Javier was a bit hesitant but let his hand be guided deep within Buster's dense feathers.

'Don't worry,' Carter assured him, 'Buster likes to be tickled here.' Soon all the others did the same.

'How does he swim?' one of the children asked.

Carter stuck out his two hands with two fingers pointing forward and waved them up and down. 'He doesn't swim like this; he'll get nowhere.' He then put his hands to his chest and waved his elbows out around him. 'He does it like this.'

Javier nodded. 'Ahh –
that's much better.'

'Dwarf Tyrants live on small
islands, so they only grow this size,'
Carter continued. 'They swim very
well and eat stinky fish. That's why people
are generally safe around him.'

'I would rather play with your tyrant than the brachio.'
Javier motioned towards Budge, who was being a bit left
out. 'They are very dangerous – they may not bite, but
they can crush you!' Javier said cautiously.

Carter could feel Javier's reluctance to get close to
Bea's new saur, which was understandable given what had
happened to his father, so he devised a game to help them

bond, involving at first jumping, then being lifted, in and out of the tree by Budge to jump in the pond, and then sliding in from Budge's long neck. As the sun got hotter Buster, who felt the heat more being jet black, dozed under the tree. The children took advantage of this by inventing a game of dare, where they crept up and had to tickle the sleeping tyrant's belly with long grass stalks. Every now and then, Buster would roll over or scratch himself mid-dream, which sent them all running with laughter.

Carter could see that Buster was happily occupied with the children, so he turned his attention to Budge, who kept his head lowered to the ground, pushing the dirt around. He pushed away a fallen log to reveal softer moist ground below it. He dipped lower and snorted from his brow nostrils, driving off the leaves, and again inspected the ground. Whatever he was looking for was not there either.

Carter, seeing that Buster was happy playing with the others, felt the need to pay closer attention to the punk, and ran his hands down Budge's flank and along his barrel-like belly. From within he felt a bubble of gas move around. At the same time he felt his own belly gargle, which rose and formed a burp that he let out loudly. Hearing this, Budge swung his head round and nudged Carter's belly gently, and in that moment they connected.

Poppo Miguel had also heard Carter's burp, and made his way over carefully.

'Budge has too much food in his belly,' Carter said as Poppo came closer. 'He wants me to find smooth stones for him to eat.'

'How do you know this?' asked Poppo in amazement. 'You are right about the stones. But how did you work it out?'

Carter shrugged, then realised the old man could not see this. 'I just know,' he said. 'Budge told me.'

'Stones help the saurs mash the vegetation in their stomachs,' Poppo Miguel explained. 'But they pass through them, so they need to keep finding new ones to swallow.'

Carter looked around and found a stone about the size of an apple that had no sharp edges. He placed it in Poppo Miguel's hand. 'Like this?' he asked.

Poppo Miguel felt it and smiled. 'Perfect. A few more like that will do.'

Carter scrambled around and found three more.

'You're a fast learner,' Poppo Miguel said. 'Now, wrap them in palm leaves so they taste a little better.'

Carter bound them up and fed them to Budge, who swallowed and lifted his head up to the sky as far as it would go to let gravity do the rest.

'Only an experienced Brachio Herder would know that his saur needed stones,' Poppo Miguel said slowly, resting a hand on Carter's shoulder as the boy led him back to the house. 'You have a remarkable gift.'

✦ ✦ ✦

After lunch, Theodore and Bea ventured back to town in order to see if Lambert had returned, and to fetch some supplies for Lucia to save her the trip. She'd been reluctant to have her guests do chores on her behalf, but Theodore insisted. Bea was given a list and off they went.

'What the –?' Theodore uttered when he took a look at the list. 'None of this makes any sense. I don't want to disappoint our hostess, but it seems we'll return empty-handed.'

'Show it to me,' Bea said. But instead of expressing puzzlement, the corner of her mouth turned up until she sported a Cheshire cat-sized grin. 'Don't you worry,' she assured him, 'leave this to me.'

Bea and Theodore made their way to the Hotel Espléndido. A charm offensive was in order to restore Theodore in the hotel manager's good graces. Theodore was recognised the moment he walked in, and had gone no more than a few steps inside the lobby when the hotel manager approached him briskly.

'About the unfortunate incident –' Theodore began, but he was cut off.

'Señor Viscount Knútr has returned,' the hotel manager snapped. 'He has asked to meet with you at the first opportunity. I trust you are alone?' He glanced over Theodore's shoulder to see if any saurs had been left outside.

'Just me and the young lady!' Theodore replied brightly, squashing Bea to him rather awkwardly with a wide smile.

The hotel manager did not smile back. 'The señor and señorita will kindly wait here,' he directed, and returned to his desk, motioning an errand boy to his side.

◆ ◆ ◆

'Theodore Logan, my dear friend!' Lambert exclaimed when he emerged a while later, and shook his hand. 'And Bea! How wonderful that you made it. But where is young Carter? He is well, I hope?'

'Absolutely,' Theodore replied.

'I understand from the manager that you're not staying at the hotel?' Lambert pressed. 'There was some sort of mix-up, perhaps?'

'Indeed,' Theodore replied wryly. 'But it's all fine now. We're staying out of town with some friends.'

'I see,' Lambert said. 'I wasn't aware you knew anybody in this particular area?'

'They're quite new friends,' Theodore responded. 'The children do like to keep company with others their own age.'

'Of course, of course,' Lambert uttered.

'How is your wife finding the climate?' Theodore asked. 'I must say I don't understand how women can wear furs in this heat, but they do.' He motioned to an elegant guest who strolled past with a fox stole about her shoulders.

'Oh, Anya cannot tolerate the tropics for any reason,' Lambert replied. 'She has wisely decided to go on a shopping spree in Europe instead.'

'I'm sure she's very happy doing that,' Bea replied politely, remembering how much Anya Stitz had enjoyed shopping in San Francisco. The trip had left Bea feeling uncomfortable as Anya had seemed to imply Bea's life with Theodore was not all it should be. She shook it from her mind.

'Nothing gives her greater pleasure,' Lambert replied. 'I'm sorry I was not here when you arrived; I was called away on an urgent business trip. Now that I'm back, why don't you all come to the hotel for dinner and stay on? I'm sure I asked the manager to find stables for the tyrant. You've purchased the provisions you'll need to head into the jungle, I trust?'

Theodore scratched his chin as they sought out the lounge. 'Not exactly,' he replied. 'And I'm afraid you may have a hard time persuading the manager to allow us to stay. He banned us because Bea's punk brachio created a disturbance on the steps.'

'Excuse me, a punk brachio?' Lambert asked.

'I'm afraid that's not all,' Theodore confessed. 'We encountered some, er, unexpected expenses along the way down here, and we've found that it's harder to find accommodations with not one, but two large saurs.' He took a deep breath. 'The truth is, Lambert, we're broke.'

'*Two* saurs, now?' Lambert said, forcing a grin. 'The money's not a problem. I can make up for your expenses. I'll have my banker give you what you need.' He gestured for a messenger and gave him brief directions and a tip. The lad sped off. 'But tell me, the lost city – are you any closer to finding its location?'

'Well, as you know, we only have the part of the map that depicts part of the jungle,' Theodore explained, 'and we also have it on good authority that it is teeming with dangerous Rebels and that all sorts of dubious things are going on in there. 'The children are eager to go in, but I have to be more careful. I can still hear Bunty telling me what to do in my head.'

'Theo!' Bea interrupted. 'That's what we came for!'

'You're right to be cautious,' Lambert agreed. 'I had the opportunity to ask the interior minister for some maps of the area as I'm surveying the land for some real estate.' He reached into his briefcase and withdrew one of them, spreading it out on the table where they sat. 'This is where we are –' he tapped the map – 'and here is where I am told the Rebels are camped out. I've marked it out in red so that you can avoid it.'

'That's very helpful,' Theodore said.

'Whatever you do, don't stray into their territory,' Lambert insisted. 'I have enough on my conscience having led Franklin and Grace to their deaths in Aru, and abandoning Carter when he was a baby. It's the least I can do to ensure your safety now. You can trust that I have everyone's well-being at heart.'

'Well, this changes things,' Theodore said, nodding slowly. 'Perhaps we should venture on with this map. I swear to you and dear Bunty up there –' he pointed to the heavens – 'we won't go anywhere near it. Promise.'

'Good,' Lambert replied. 'Now, look – marked in green are places the government have already mapped, so we know the lost city can't be there.'

'That narrows it down a lot,' Theodore said. 'Well done, Lambert – this is the break we need.'

'Excellent,' Lambert grinned. 'Oh – and before I forget, I have some tickets to the Gemini Festival for you and the children for when you return. It's quite a big deal around here. These are for the VIP area alongside the president!'

'How splendid!' Bea said with a broad smile, imagining the spectacle that the Canteras had described. 'We will absolutely love that!'

'How about a drink?' Lambert sat back and smiled. 'The *mezcal* is a local speciality –' and nodding at Bea – 'as is the lemonade.'

The waiter brought the drinks. 'To your success,' Lambert proposed.

'To our success,' Theodore added, and knocked back the *mezcal*. 'Whoa!' he wheezed, clutching his throat as the fiery liquid scalded its way down. 'This stuff's strong!'

◆ ◆ ◆

They left the hotel with a renewed spring in their step – but Theodore had one more task to accomplish before they headed back to the Canteras'. So they parted ways, and with cash in her pocket Bea went off to do the shopping as Theodore headed towards the large white municipal building that housed both the mayor's office and the police department.

Like the hotel, it was fronted by a set of sweeping steps that separated everything and everyone inside from the daily life of ordinary citizens. At the entrance stood two men in uniform. Theodore tucked in his shirt, and for the first time in years did up his top button and smoothed down his foppish hair before approaching them.

'Excuse me,' he said in a refined English accent, 'I'm here to see the mayor.'

One of the guards asked him what business he had that required such a meeting, and Theodore told them that he had information about some dubious activities at the avocado plantation. The guard was not prepared to let in just anyone, so Theodore waited patiently in the sunshine to be admitted, fiddling with his top button as from the first-floor window the other guard could be seen pointing to Theodore below.

'That looks like him,' said the mayor, hanging back from the window so he could not be seen.

General Vulpez took his place to get a good look at him. 'Are you sure?' he asked. 'Without a doubt?'

'He brought a tyrant and a punk brachio into town and nearly destroyed the market. He was asking at the hotel for our friend, the Viscount,' the mayor said, raising his eyebrows. 'He was thrown out before the manager could learn any more. Made a right mess of the place.'

'Good work,' the General said without looking at the mayor. 'Leave the questioning to me.'

◆ ◆ ◆

'Good morning,' General Vulpez said as Theodore was led to his office and they shook hands. 'I am General Vulpez. I'm afraid the mayor is in a meeting. Can I be of assistance?'

The General listened politely as Theodore told him what he had 'overheard' about the dark going-ons at the avocado plantation, which he suspected could be a front for illegal logging or something worse. Theodore was

careful not to mention Lucia's involvement, even though the General kept pushing for more information. He remained deliberately vague. Lucia had seemed scared of something, and so he didn't want to betray her trust.

'Thank you, Mr Logan,' General Vulpez said eventually. 'If only all our citizens were as honest as you! Are you staying for the Gemini Festival?'

'I think we will,' Theodore replied. 'It sounds like quite a party!'

'Oh it certainly is,' the General said as they shook hands once again. 'And remember, if you hear more, do come back and speak directly to me.'

◆ ◆ ◆

'What did he say?' asked the mayor when General Vulpez returned.

'Enough to know he's a troublemaker.'

'What shall we do?' said the mayor. 'He could ruin all our plans.'

'Don't worry,' the General said. 'My men will make sure he gets the message that he's not wanted around here.' He flicked his cigar out of the window and it landed halfway down the white steps below and rolled down the rest towards the iron railings. One of the guards turned round, and the General gave him a nod and pointed to Theodore walking away.

10

The Unwelcome Guests

~ FIRE! ~

'After the "long weight" the man in the shop was happy to sell me these seven pots of "rainbow paint" – red, orange, yellow, green, blue, indigo and violet.' Bea smiled at Lucia and theatrically placed all seven tins of paint onto the table. 'And the helpful man said he could also get archery lube to grease a bow, but he says this stuff –' she put down a small pot of lanolin – 'will do fine, no need for any costly "El Bow Grease".'

Lucia started to laugh but Theodore stopped her. Bea was not done yet.

'The next thing on the list was a little tricky to get, but I found a stall in the market selling beauty products and, sure enough, they had a variety of ladies' nail files. This one is a lot better than the rest, as it has glass fragments embedded in it. It's a "glass nail" file.'

Lucia could not contain her laughter. When she calmed down Theodore finished up with the last thing on the shopping list.

'Finally, this pencil is much better than the "left-handed pencil" you wanted.' He waved it about in front of her and then popped it into his other hand. 'Look – it can be used in both left and right hands!'

Theodore grinned from ear to ear. 'I could never have done it without Bea,' he explained. 'We met Lambert at the hotel. Here is your money back, Lucia – and some extra for your hospitality.'

'Oh wonderful!' Carter exclaimed. 'Can we go and see him?'

'Sorry, Carter – he had to go away again, but we're meeting him at the Gemini Festival.' He showed them the tickets. 'He gave me these – and the president will be there!'

The children jumped up and down with joy.

'I also have other news,' Theodore said brightly, holding up the map. 'Lambert has been doing his research – look at this!' He unfolded it and pointed out the red and green areas.

Lucia tapped the red area. 'That's where the avocado plantation is.'

'It looks like your former employers are up to no good,' Theodore concurred. 'Lambert was told on good authority that it was a Rebel-held area. I'm glad you have nothing more to do with it.'

Bea perused the map closely. She was reminded of her time in Kenya with that horrible man Christian Hayter watching over her while she had to break the code hidden on the playing cards. Something was familiar yet out of place, and she couldn't figure it out. But then it occurred to her. She pulled from her satchel her father's journal, and opened it alongside the new one she had been working in. While Lucia prepared dinner and Theodore put away all the pots of paint she pondered over her notes.

'Theo, remember the description we found at the saur graveyard of how the twins got there from the lost city? The one we translated from the carvings in the wall?' Bea finally said.

'Yes,' he replied, 'but it's not much help – it's not a map like this one.' He tapped the table and winked proudly.

'Well, it is sort of a map,' Bea reasoned. 'After all, we followed the description all the way back to here.'

'I guess so,' he replied. 'What are you getting at?'

Bea located a page in her journal and read out the first part describing the twins leaving the city. 'Five days' walk from the city until we left the trees . . .' She looked up at Theodore. 'How far is five days' walk in a dense jungle?'

'Mmmm.' Theodore looked at the map. 'I see your point.' He ran his finger along a wide perimeter of the jungle's interior. 'I would hazard a guess about there.' His shoulders slumped, deflated. 'Oh dear. It's going to be an impossible task to cover that amount of ground.'

Bea smiled at him. 'But this is an old map and the edge of the jungle is constantly receding as people cut it back for farmland – that was what Poppo Miguel said, wasn't it? Over two thousand years ago the jungle probably came right up to the town. Where we are now was once probably two or three days' walk into the jungle.'

'If that's the case, then five days' walk would be here,' Theodore said, stabbing his finger into the map, 'not nearly as far into the jungle from here as it seemed.' Theodore patted Bea on the back. 'You are a clever thing! Well done! Let's head off in a few days to see what we can find – and keep well away from the Rebels.' He smiled at her. 'Your father would have been so proud.'

'And my mother?' Bea teased.

'Grace, Franklin and Bunty, bless them all,' Theodore said, and gave his god-daughter a hug.

Pleased as she was with Theodore's praise, Bea couldn't help but remain troubled.

✦ ✦ ✦

Over dinner that evening Lucia explained her prank on Bea and Theodore, causing Poppo Miguel to giggle well into the night. Theodore insisted that they had no intention of intruding on the Cantera family any more than they had already, and that he, Bea and Carter would be happy to sleep under the tree behind the house below the stars. It would also mean they could keep an eye on Budge and Buster. Carter explained he always slept with Buster, even back home, and Bea remarked how comfortable Javier's hammock in the tree was. Theodore promised to look after them all and make sure Budge would behave and not wander off for a midnight feast, as the young brachio had already been busy keeping all the plants he could reach very well trimmed.

In the early hours of the morning, Bea was woken from her sleep in the tree by a violent knocking at the door of the Canteras' house. Men in military uniforms were demanding to know where the Rebels were hiding. Lucia joined Javier at the door, protesting as the men barged in and searched the house, turning everything over and trashing the place. The commotion had everyone awake by now, and from her vantage point up high, Bea could hear that nothing Lucia said satisfied them. Behind the house, in the tree, Bea and Carter kept as quiet as mice, their hearts beating wildly. Theodore, woken from his slumber by the saurs on the ground, motioned for the children to stay where they were, readying himself, knife in hand. He was about to burst in the back door when Poppo Miguel, standing near a window, quickly waved him away. Before Theodore could question how on earth Poppo Miguel could tell he was there, two of the men came out, kicked over a few barrels to see what was in them, and then left to cause more grief inside.

When they finally left, having found nothing, Bea climbed down from the tree. Lucia was in tears, Javier consoling her. Poppo Miguel opened the back door, held his finger to his lips at all the assembled company, and waved for Lucia and Javier to join him outside.

Theodore led Poppo Miguel by the hand round the pond to the tree before anyone spoke.

'What just happened?' whispered Bea.

'I don't understand,' Lucia wept. 'Why would the army accuse my husband of having been a Rebel? He's been dead for five years now!'

Then, before anyone could speak, a bright flash lit the windows from inside the house. They heard the sound of glass smashing.

'Oh no, oh no, oh no,' Bea moaned – then at the top of her lungs she yelled out, 'FIRE!'

Javier ran towards the house but the bone-dry wood was already ablaze. The flames took hold quickly and soon the whole house was engulfed. Their frantic shouts of 'FIRE! FIRE' had brought all the villagers out of their homes in a hurry. They formed a line from the pond, passing buckets and pans of water to try to douse it, but it wasn't the kind of fire that sometimes flared up on a too-hot stove or a tipped candle; this fire spread too quickly, and burned too hot. It had been fuelled by gasoline.

Suddenly a staccato *pop, pop, pop* rang through the air. Budge and Buster were frantic, and it took all of Bea's and Carter's strength to pull them away from danger, and to create space for those fighting the fire to work. Carter shook from the fear he felt raging inside the saurs, while Bea trembled uncontrollably for another reason.

'Why are they shooting?' Bea sobbed, flinching as another shot sounded.

'It's okay, Bea.' Theodore was by her side, passing his full bucket of water forward and then holding her to comfort her. 'It's just the paint tins exploding. It will be okay, I promise. Everyone is safe, Bea. Everyone is safe.'

For Bea, though, there was little comfort to be had, as the sights and sounds took her back to the night her beloved grandmother had been killed in the fire that had swept through their lodge in Kenya. The intense heat, the smoke and the flames made her painfully aware of how much danger they were all in as the relentless fire consumed the building.

On and on they fought, Javier holding his mother back to prevent her from rushing into their home to rescue treasured items despite the sizzling heat. Poppo Miguel

remained at the pond filling anything and everything that
was handed to him and passing it along to waiting hands.
The fire burned fierce and
quick, and by the time dawn's
earliest rays glowed red
beyond the smoke it
had burned itself out.
Exhausted, everyone
slumped on the
ground, and

because there were no words that could possibly make it better they listened to the crackle and snap of embers consuming themselves. It was a wretched scene. The fire, having arrived so soon upon the heels of the raid, could not have been a coincidence.

Lucia sat in Javier's arms stunned. 'Why?' he asked. 'Why would the army want to kill us? What have we done?'

As they picked through the smouldering ruins, wondering what they could do, Javier spoke again. 'Let's leave, Mama. Let's go far away from here, so that the army can never do it again.' He sounded scared. He'd already lost so much in his young life, and even though their neighbours had all jumped in to help he'd heard them whispering to each other about the Canteras being bad luck.

'Where can we go, Javier?' Lucia said wearily. 'There's nowhere to go.'

'We cannot remain here,' Poppo Miguel decided. 'Javier's right. It would be best to lie low for a while. And I know of a place we can go – where I was raised.'

'But the jungle is dangerous,' Lucia protested in anguish.

'There's safety in numbers,' Poppo Miguel assured her. 'And Theodore's friend has told him where the Rebels are, so we can avoid them.'

'But how will you know where you're going?' Lucia asked. 'It's been many years since you were there, and you cannot see.'

The old man nodded. 'I don't need to see. The girl has a map,' he said.

So they gathered whatever they could and, taking turns riding and walking alongside Budge and Buster, cautiously made their way into the jungle. The last leg of their journey had begun, whether they liked it or not.

11

The Irritators

~ a one-two punch ~

The mayor liked to travel in style, but he could not risk his official and expensive vehicle, a visible symbol of his ill-gained wealth, being seen anywhere near the Rebels' camp. His driver was instructed to park it at the edge of a reputable neighbourhood before transferring him into an unmarked car, and then, at the edge of the jungle, changing finally into a third truck driven by General Vulpez.

They pulled into a clearing and came to a stop outside the low wooden building. General Vulpez ushered him inside.

'Señor Mayor, let me present Doctor Klaus Achtecka; he's in charge of the new tritops from America. And this is Mr Christian Hayter, who is helping oversee our saurs' welfare and security.'

The General smirked at Hayter's job description as everyone shook hands.

'Your work here is impressive,' the mayor announced. 'I trust the Viscount is pleased with your progress? I thought he would be here.'

'He's out with my men inspecting the Irritators we rounded up,' Hayter replied.

The mayor popped a fresh cigar in his mouth and lit it. 'I wanted to see him,' he announced curtly, addressing both men. 'It seems that some friends of his are also in this area. Did you know about this? I do not like surprises. One of them came snooping around my office wanting to reveal information that would have ended our business

here if he had spoken to the wrong people.'

'I do not know who you mean,' the Doctor replied. 'Perhaps you can describe him?'

'A *gringo*, like Mr Hayter here. He was apparently travelling with two children, one who was riding a brachio, and one on a Black Tyrant.' The mayor puffed away, letting smoke coil up into the air.

'Theodore Logan!' Hayter exclaimed, shock punctuating his voice. 'Here?'

'So you do know him.' The mayor flicked his ash onto the table and blew smoke in the Doctor's face.

'Perhaps,' the Doctor answered cautiously, wafting the smoke away and shooting a look at Hayter, 'they are just old friends of the Viscount, not friends of ours.'

'Well, the man seemed to know a lot about the goings-on at our avocado plantation, and he was not being discreet about it. Luckily he spoke to the General here. If it had been the police chief we would not be having this conversation.' The mayor's face reddened with anger.

'I had him followed,' said General Vulpez, who leant in close. 'He went to the home of someone who used to work here. So we had no choice but to return that night and discipline the traitor who had informed him. Otherwise the farm workers here would not respect the rules of their employment.'

'And Logan, what did you do with him?' Hayter asked.

'He and the children were not there when we returned. General Vulpez here was friendly enough to him – we'll bring him in for questioning when he shows up again,' the mayor said.

'I was in favour of killing them all, but the mayor here insisted he wanted to find out how they are involved with you all first,' the General added.

'Well, I would have helped you kill them,' Hayter blurted out, but the Doctor held onto his arm to stop him saying any more.

'With all due respect, Señor Mayor,' the Doctor urged, 'we must tread lightly. The Viscount must have something in mind involving Mr Logan, and it would not be wise to upset his plans.'

'What about upsetting my plans?' the mayor replied, and got up to leave. 'Let me remind you all of the risk we are taking in this venture. I pray the reward outweighs it!' He stormed outside, General Vulpez following, leaving the Doctor and Hayter looking at each other.

'Did you know about this?' Hayter spat as soon as the visitors were gone.

'No,' the Doctor replied. 'But I have a good idea what Mr Logan's intentions are. We must be careful, Mr Hayter. I will have a quiet word with Herr Viscount later.'

All of a sudden a loud whistle blew twice – the code for a predator nearby. Before anyone moved Hayter darted outside and leapt upon Buttercup to find the source of the threat. The mayor, meanwhile, hunkered down behind a table as a reflex. It didn't take long; all he had to do was listen for gunshots. When he got to the next circular clearing they found some of the General's men firing at an enormous titanosaur, which was sizing up an even bigger chained brachio. The titanosaur held his head low to the ground, letting its thick tail wave up in the air behind it, sending waves rippling down the extended spines along its back. The brachio was doing the opposite, lowering its tail to the ground to support its front legs as it raised them in self-defence. Their bullets were no match for the angry saur; all they seemed to do was make it more angry. It turned and roared at the guards, sending them all scattering as far back as they could. The brachio reared back and up on its hind legs and supported itself with its huge tail as it waved its front legs erratically towards its attacker. It honked so loudly that the sound bounced back and forth across the clearing, making everyone's ears ring. Honks from other brachios, each in their own circular prison, called back, sending all the wildlife scattering out of the trees in fright.

The titanosaur repositioned itself to the side of its prey, swinging its tail. The brachio tipped forward and thumped its front legs to the ground with such force that a large fallen tree splintered to bits under its huge feet.

Fighting for its life, the brachio was a force to be reckoned with, its own tail slashing from side to side as

it took down two smaller trees in one go. It tugged at its chain and turned to face the titanosaur once again. The Doctor had now caught up with Hayter on the edge of the clearing, and was holding his bag of surgical equipment.

'A perfect specimen,' he muttered to himself. 'Where is the Viscount?'

Hayter turned round and caught a glint of light high up in a tree behind them. 'He's

in position for the kill.' He nodded towards the hide they had made for just this purpose.

'Good. We need to earn some trust from our hosts. I wish that I could help you,' the Doctor said, adjusting the dark round glasses that had slipped a little from the sweat dripping off his face, 'but you will have to do this on your own.'

Hayter nodded back. 'I've got this covered. Tell Ash and Bishop to release the Irritators!'

◆ ◆ ◆

General Vulpez arrived on foot after rallying his guards to protect the mayor, who eventually caught up, huffing and puffing. His curiosity had evidently got the better of him.

'General!' Hayter shouted out boldly. 'Call your men off!'

'Don't be stupid,' the mayor spat. 'How are you going to do what several of the General's guards can't?'

'No – look.' The Doctor smiled. 'Just watch the expert at work.' He headed back out to the Irritators' pen. 'Release them!' he commanded.

Ash grinned broadly as he unlatched the makeshift pen, revealing his secret weapon: a keystone set into one of his teeth, which gave him a sparkling smile. Putting two fingers into his mouth, he issued a set of whistles a shepherd might use with his sheepdogs. All at once, the Irritators gathered together and became extremely alert. Ash gave a few more whistles, which seemed somehow amplified by the opal keystone, and out they ran from the pen and over towards the circular clearing where all the commotion was.

'Irritators!' the mayor cried, pointing and laughing out loud as they ran into the clearing and stopped, taking in the huge bulk of the brachio and the titanosaur facing each other off. On their own or as a pack they were no match for the titanosaur and would never attack in the wild. But now, rather than instinctively running away, they held their ground.

As soon as Ash let out a clean shrill whistle they all moved round the perimeter of the clearing and got between the brachio and the titanosaur, forming a barrier, their splayed teeth dripping with saliva, all intently staring at the enormous carnivore with their deranged acid-green eyes.

'Good, keep it from escaping!' Hayter called out to Bishop as he rode into the clearing on Buttercup. A few Irritators became skittish as the gnashing titanosaur came close to them and let out a chilling roar, but another amplified whistle from Ash steadied them. As soon as the titanosaur was pushed away from the brachio Hayter held his bullhook aloft and pointed it in the enormous saur's direction, and with another long, shrill whistle all the Irritators attacked at once. The titanosaur looked more confused than the mayor or General Vulpez. It could never have imagined that Irritators would attempt to attack it.

'How on earth –' the mayor muttered.

The Irritators were being driven by something greater than instinct and were being controlled or commanded to do the task. It did not mean they did a good job of it, however, far from it. The Irritators had no form; they only bothered and distracted the titanosaur with snaps from their long thin snouts, which had evolved to catch small prey. Their claws looked impressive but they were used for digging and scratching away rotten wood to get to hiding rodents, so the titanosaur's thick hide was ample protection against them. The puzzled titanosaur swiped, bit and tore into the pack like a professional beating away unwanted attention from amateurs.

With the predator distracted Bishop crept round the outer edge towards the brachio, who was trying to get as far away as possible from all the carnivores while still defensively rearing up onto its back legs and then stomping down.

The General pointed to Bishop. 'What is that fool doing?'

Hayter's bulky henchman approached the frenzied brachio purposefully, rolling up his sleeves. He pulled from his pocket a knuckleduster with a sparkling keystone set into it and jammed it onto his hand. The saur's dangerous tail thrashed and took out another tree as it reared up its huge mass yet again, and craned its head low to issue another long ear-splitting honk. Hayter immediately trotted in front of it and held out his bullhook so that the shafts of daylight streaming into the clearing dazzled the keystone set within it. The brachio caught sight of this and abruptly stopped its honk midway, lowered its front legs to the ground, and gaped silently at it.

'Good, Bishop,' Hayter called out. 'Now if you would be so kind as to make it sit and stay still, I can prepare the other saur for its fate.'

With the brachio distracted Bishop had positioned himself directly in front of the enormous creature. He nodded to his boss and turned to deliver a powerful punch upwards right to its chest. The brachio startled and dropped its head to give this new attacker a closer look. Bishop took a slight step back, then swung his arm once more to punch the brachio on the nose. The blow was not enough to harm it – but it was stunned into submission and calmly retreated to the length of its chain and sat down quivering.

The General's mouth dropped and out of it fell the cigar he was smoking.

The mayor tried to say something but was dumbstruck at the way such a large saur could be brought under control by such a simple gesture.

The titanosaur, meanwhile, was growing tired of battering the Irritators away. Its chest was inflating and deflating rapidly and it was panting hard. At Hayter's command Ash let rip another whistle, making the Irritators stop and retreat to the edge of the clearing, exhausted. One was already dead, another fell to the ground and died on the spot from a nasty bite, while another limped badly and only just made it back to the edge with the others.

Ash grinned a sparkling smile back at his boss.

The titanosaur turned to face Hayter astride his tyrant, Buttercup, who trotted round its formidable opponent, sizing it up and leaning in for the occasional snap and menacing roar.

'Shall I take him, Viscount?' Hayter shouted.

The mayor and General Vulpez looked around, but the Viscount was nowhere to be seen.

Suddenly a single gunshot rang out from behind them. For a moment everything stood still, then, like a tree falling, the titanosaur tilted backwards – slowly at first, and then picking up speed as it crashed to the ground, sending up an almighty cloud of dirt.

Hayter ambled up and admired the single clean shot that had taken it out.

The Doctor turned and nodded to the Viscount, who was climbing down from his vantage point in the tree. 'Good shot,' he remarked as the Viscount came towards him, handing over the rifle.

'And now please remove its head,' the Viscount instructed. 'It will make a fine addition to my collection.'

'Certainly,' replied the Doctor. 'I have my equipment here to extract its glands as well.' He tapped his bag.

'Good,' the Viscount murmured.

'Señor Viscount!' The General approached with the mayor, dabbing his brow from the heat. 'A word, please.'

The Viscount pointedly ignored them both and strolled over towards Hayter, who was presiding over the slain titanosaur. 'Well done, Mr Hayter,' he offered warmly. 'You lined me up a perfect shot. It was the best kill to date, even better than the White Titan Tyrant sitting on its nest in Kenya!' He smiled as the Doctor walked round and marvelled at the dead saur.

'My pleasure,' he said, and tapped Buttercup on the neck, 'but we could have taken it.'

'I'm glad you left that for me,' the Viscount said, pointing to the injured Irritator laying close by, which was making a gurgling cry as it slowly died in pain. 'Silence it,' he ordered.

'Señor Viscount!' the General called out again, but was ignored as Hayter trotted past them and approached the Irritator, who'd got the wrong end of the titanosaur's tail and lay trembling on the ground. Hayter dismounted and patted Buttercup, who'd been waiting patiently. 'Din-dins!' he chimed.

With that the hungry Mountain Lythronax pounced and tore away at the titanosaur's neck.

12

Answers to Difficult Questions

~ a risky gamble ~

The Viscount stood on the barrel chest of the slain titanosaur to get a better view of General Vulpez and the mayor heading back to town. He knew they were well aware of him bearing down on them and stood fast as they disappeared from the clearing in the old truck.

'Hayter's masterclass in dominating the wild saurs had a great effect on them,' purred the Doctor.

'You did well training him,' the Viscount added as he finally turned and faced the Doctor. 'Though it would have been better had you revealed your talents. Are the Saurmen stones not good enough for you?' He stepped down from the titanosaur and stood to watch the man in black work.

The Doctor paused, took a black rubber glove off his hand, and lifted his dark glasses from his face to reveal the hole where his opal eye once dazzled and spread fear into every saur that saw it.

'I have tried them all.' The Doctor sighed. 'Sadly it has to be a perfect fit for me to connect with it. I fear that finding a replacement is impossible. Hayter and his men will have to do.'

The Viscount stared into the empty socket. 'But the impossible *is* possible.' He smiled as the man replaced his spectacles and pulled his glove back on. 'Do you have what you need?'

'Yes,' the Doctor replied. 'Let's take this back to my laboratory while it's still fresh.'

✦ ✦ ✦

'Forgive me for intruding, Herr Viscount,' said the Doctor once they were alone. 'I sense that your reasons for being here in the jungle are more than just farming tritops.' He pointed a blood-soaked gloved finger towards a collection of clean glass jars. 'Would you be ever so kind and pass me one of those?'

'I did everything I could to prevent Mr Logan from sniffing out our presence here,' the Viscount huffed, handing over the jar. 'Trust him to befriend a disgruntled worker. I do hope he can continue with the task I have given him – it is of the utmost importance he succeeds.' The Viscount was still irritated at the incessant questioning by the mayor and Vulpez about his involvement with Logan and the Kingsley children. He had dismissed their worries with well-thought-out answers, including that

Mr Logan was just an acquaintance passing through, and reassured them that he couldn't possibly know about their involvement with the 'avocado plantation'; clearly he was merely passing on gossip he had heard on his journey, and now that he had done his duty in informing the authorities he would forget it. He had also warned them that perhaps Mr Logan had got his information from one of their loose-lipped employees.

'I assume you want him to use his abilities to find something?' the Doctor enquired. 'I understand there is no greater treasure than the fabled lost city rumoured to be in this jungle.'

'Correct,' said the Viscount. 'You are astute, Doctor. I've known for some time the city is located somewhere near here.' He opened his top pocket and pulled out three pieces of paper, each torn down one edge and covered with writing and drawings. 'This tritop enterprise is very important for my business but it also benefits my personal interests, giving me a legitimate reason to be here looking for the Saurman city. When I first approached the president he declined my offer, but luckily the General had no problem with the deforestation of the pristine jungle around us.' He folded the papers again before the Doctor could examine them. 'When Theodore Logan demonstrated how good he was at using his keystone and finding Saurman temples in California I had to gently persuade him to find this place for me.' The Viscount pondered. 'Further still, the boy may be of use and I would like to be here to oversee things.'

'The lure of all that gold waiting to be found is too irresistible,' agreed the Doctor, looking up.

'Actually the gold is just a nice thing to have on the side. I have a different motive,' the Viscount said. 'You see my old friends, Franklin and Grace, discovered that keystones don't just come from the lightning fields in Australia. There are other places in the world where opal is found.' He gestured with a sweeping hand to the deep green of the jungle that surrounded the clearing. 'The ancient people who once ruled this land not only decorated things in gold, but also set into them many semi-precious stones like jade, lapis and

opal. Over the years I have acquired some of these artefacts and discovered that these opals have the properties I'm interested in. Some were once dinosaur bones, and these are the ones that Saurmen use to channel their powers.' The Viscount grinned.

'How do you know all this?' asked the Doctor. He passed the glass jar now containing some sort of titanosaur bodily fluid back to the Viscount. 'I will need one more jar please; there is a lot to drain from this gland.'

The Viscount obliged and continued his explanation. 'Franklin told me some of it, and I read the rest in his journal,' he explained. 'I tore the pages detailing this out before I gave the journal to Mr Logan.' The Viscount tapped his top pocket. 'Naturally I had to convey the information in these pages back to Theodore on another map, so he wouldn't know it was me who took the pages.' He paused. 'I made it very clear that he was to keep out of the areas marked in red, and General Vulpez has done a good job of making sure no one dares go near this place,' he mused. 'Anyway, it is believed the ancient kings used the Saurmen to help corral the wild saurs to clear the jungle terraces so that the city could be built around the sources of these minerals. They traded some of the gold and stones. All we know of this city is from the few artefacts they took with them. Then one day it all stopped. We don't know exactly when, or why, but the kingdom fell and the city became lost for ever.'

'And you think Logan can find it – a city lost for thousands of years?' asked the Doctor incredulously.

The Viscount smiled. 'It's a Saurman city riddled with sparkling keystones. If anyone can find it, Mr Logan can. He proved that to me back in America, at the saur graveyard. But that's not all,' he continued. 'He also believes he found there a crude description of the twins' journey – a description which leads back here to their birthplace, the lost city. They were going to find a way to get here eventually. He is now on a mission to finish off the Kingsleys' work so I thought it best to use the opportunity to help them find it.'

'This is a risky gamble, Herr Viscount,' the Doctor said, shaking his head, and in doing so he glanced down and stepped away from a growing puddle of blood on the ground. 'Keeping Logan and those children from discovering your other interests in this jungle could prove tricky. What if the General finds out the truth, that you are sending them to discover the lost city and find gold?'

'That might be true,' the Viscount pondered, 'but one way or another General Vulpez will probably be the next president of this country. Helping him get what he wants, means we get what *we* want.'

'And what is that, Herr Viscount?' the Doctor questioned. 'The gold? Is my work for you in glandular extracts and selective breeding not enough? Why is it you let these Kingsley people into your life? The brachios here can be used to find your lost city without the need for Logan's alleged Saurman abilities.'

The Viscount smiled. 'I'm after something far more valuable than gold. If I locate a source of these opalised dinosaur bones, then I can build an elite army to support my numerous ventures.' He pointed over to where Hayter, Ash and Bishop were herding the remaining Irritators into their pen. 'Many more men like Mr Hayter and those

other two chaps can be trained by you to command saurs to fight for us.' He chuckled to himself. 'You see, my dear Doctor, I'm not interested in the Saurmen – they are just a defunct band of medicine men swallowed up by history. But I *am* fascinated to understand the powers they had – and how to harness them.'

'So if Logan finds the lost city, then what?'

'Then they shall be of no further use to me, and I'll get rid of them of course.' The Viscount inspected the lapel of his pristine suit and dusted away a fleck of pollen.

'What of the saur boy?' the Doctor persisted. 'You and Mr Hayter say he needs no keystone to yield this power, which I have seen up close – and he stole my opal eye from me; I want it back.' He adjusted his darkened glasses.

'Even more reason to let them find this city,' the Viscount replied. 'We will be able to replace your eye from the huge selection of keystones at our disposal.' The Viscount raised his eyebrows. 'Do you see my point of view now, Doctor?'

'Clearly.'

The Viscount smiled and paused for a moment before continuing. 'The boy – his condition needs to be examined carefully. He is useful to us, but we need to find a way to make him co-operate. I'm sure a solution will present itself in due course, but for now we need to make sure that the General is kept in the dark about my larger interests here. I'm due to meet Mr Logan and the children at the Gemini Festival. Hopefully they will have good news.'

✦ ✦ ✦

When the Doctor had finished dissecting the titanosaur and extracting its glands the Viscount called Hayter over to instruct him on exactly where the head should be cut from the body. Ash and Bishop were set the new task of preparing a packing case for it, made from one of the ammunition cases used for transporting the eggs.

'What is Logan doing here?' Hayter demanded, spitting on the ground.

The Viscount grimaced. 'Do you mind?' he said. 'We may be in a jungle, but I, at least, am not a savage.' He glared at Hayter then said, 'Just think of them as expendable scouts. Mr Logan has an important thing to find and then he will be removed for ever.'

'And what is so important for him to find?'

'Never mind that,' the Viscount said dismissively. 'But you might have to help point him in the right direction.'

'And how do you suppose I do that?' Hayter asked. 'I've no idea what he's looking for. Anyway, you can't send me; they know what I look like and they certainly don't trust me.'

'Which is why I shall send Ash and Bishop instead. It is imperative that Logan and the Kingsley children are not made aware of our real purpose here.'

'Understood,' Hayter noted reluctantly.

'Your two men have adapted to their new tools well,' the Viscount offered. 'I was impressed with their display earlier.'

'They have made good progress,' Hayter replied, smoothing his trusty bullhook with this thumb. 'Though it'll take them a while to catch up with me.'

'Don't get ahead of yourself, Mr Hayter. With the power I have given you comes a greater responsibility, and I expect a little more refinement and discipline, you understand?'

Hayter nodded.

'Good,' the Viscount snapped. 'Now please make a clean cut when removing the titanosaur's head.'

13

The End of the Chain

~ out of the frying pan, into the fire ~

The going was dreadfully slow. An oppressive humidity penetrated the jungle as Theodore, Bea and Carter made their way slowly along behind Poppo Miguel, Lucia and Javier. All around them rustled the leaves of bushes and trees, whose sounds competed with a cacophony of insects and birds. Poppo Miguel had instructed them to be on the lookout for colourful snakes and cleverly camouflaged beetles whose bites could prove dangerous. Yet everywhere Bea looked a flash of colour caught her eye. Sometimes it was a plume of blossom hanging from a tree; sometimes a brightly feathered bird flitting from branch to branch looking for fruit. Every now and then Carter's ears pricked up at the rustle of a creature rummaging in the undergrowth, and all his senses were engaged as he sniffed out new smells that painted a very different picture from the jungle he had grown up in on Aru. The heat filtered through the canopy causing sweat to prickle on their skin. It seemed like they followed no path, yet one always seemed to open up before them.

Poppo Miguel listened intently for clues to help guide him along, and, like Carter, constantly sniffed the air. This way he was able to avoid leading them through spiny thickets and instead into areas through which it was easier to pass.

When they stopped to rest and refill their flasks at a stream Lucia spotted Bea's silver locket and pendant swinging out from the top of her blouse as she bent down. A burst of multicoloured light flashed from it as the dancing water reflected the dappled sun from below.

'Your necklace is beautiful,' Lucia said, admiring it.

'Thank you,' Bea replied. 'It matches one my father used to have. It's very old.'

'The people from whom we are descended made great use of the precious metals and gems they mined,' Lucia said. 'Perhaps this is why the Europeans took such an interest in this part of the world.'

'It seems that some people always want what others have,' Bea said philosophically. 'On Aru, where we found Carter, traders nearly wiped out the Raptors of Paradise by killing them for their feathers – and all for fashion.'

'I've heard of those,' Lucia said. 'The rich women here like to wear exotic feathers too, and furs. They have to borrow their beauty because they can't see their own.' She gave Bea a small smile. 'That stone you wear,' she continued, 'the Mayans believed it was created in the heavens. They called it "Paradise Bird".'

'What a coincidence!' Bea exclaimed. She looked down and touched the opalised keystone that had once been worn by a long-dead twin. 'My parents were looking for Raptors of Paradise when they were killed. My mother sent me one of their feathers in the last letter she wrote to me. Now I wear a Paradise Bird next to her picture.'

'Is that who's in your locket?' Lucia asked.

Bea smiled and opened it up for her to see. 'Mummy and Daddy,' she said. 'They gave it to me before they set sail. I was just two.'

'You look just like your mother!' Lucia winked at Bea, who blushed a little. 'And I can see Carter in your father – he has the same eyes. 'You had adventurous parents!' After a pause, Lucia said, 'I'm curious – it's unusual for a girl to own a brachiosaur. How did you come by him?'

'It's a sad story,' Bea told her. 'He was abandoned by his mother. His mother died. Poachers. Illegal poachers, who left him all alone. I didn't want to leave him by the side of the road. So here he is!'

'Fascinating,' Lucia murmured. 'Where were you when this happened?'

'Oaxaca,' Bea said. 'Just outside Oaxaca.'

'I was expecting a story about how you won him at a Rodeo,' Lucia said gently. 'What's the real story, Bea?'

Bea froze. In the back of her mind she knew that she couldn't maintain a lie for ever. It wasn't like her to issue falsehoods – but then it wasn't like her to feel embarrassed by her actions either. 'You're right,' she admitted reluctantly. 'That's what I told Javier. But the truth is that I did none of those things. The truth is that I did one very stupid thing and it cost us everything we had.'

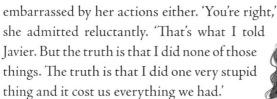

'And that's why you have no money?' Lucia gently coaxed.

'Yes,' Bea said in a small voice.

'I've done many silly things too, you know,' Lucia confided. 'Things I'm not proud of. But my mother told me it's better to own up to them and be forgiven, than keep them buried and punishing yourself.'

Bea appreciated the advice. It was times like these that she missed her own mother the most. But Lucia was a kind and generous person, and she felt she owed it to her to open up. 'I bought him,' she confessed, 'by accident. We were at an auction, and he was one of the lots. We'd seen how the brachios were used in the cruellest of ways – kept on chains, painted up with adverts for tourists in Acapulco. Lucia, they were made to stand out in the hot sun all day long! I couldn't bear it. So when his lot came up, I raised my hand. I just kept raising it. Theo and Carter were getting some corn for us to eat from one of the stalls. I think some man wanted to buy him instead, but I kept driving up the price until – well, until the hammer went down and I was his new owner. I didn't think it through; I just wanted to save him. Then the auctioneer asked for payment, and it was practically all the money we had. I begged him to let us off the hook, but he was adamant. Some very serious-looking men gathered around us until we paid, and Theo had to be very diplomatic so that we could leave safely. They didn't realise we were the ones travelling with Buster, and they backed off once we joined him and Carter. I feel like such a fool.'

Lucia pulled Bea in for a big hug. 'You were wrong,' she said.

'Don't remind me!' Bea snuffled into her shoulder.

'I mean, you were wrong about not being proud of your actions,' Lucia clarified. 'What you did was noble. It might have cost you money, but look what you got in return.' She lifted Bea's chin to see Budge happily nibbling on some leaves in the shade. 'You most probably saved his life – that's something to be proud of. Javier's father would have done the same – he loved brachios.' She looked over to her son. 'Until you came along Javier avoided saurs. Being around Budge is curing him of his fears. This is a good thing.'

Bea thought that was very kind of Lucia to say, even if she did still feel guilty for having acted impetuously. She went to say thank you, but found her voice was trapped behind an enormous lump that had appeared in her throat, and all that came out was a little air and a sob.

'It's all right,' Lucia urged. 'Sometimes it's okay to let it all out.'

Bea was more grateful than she could possibly say. A weight had been lifted that she hadn't even been aware she'd been carrying.

◆ ◆ ◆

Over supper at their camp for the night Carter asked Poppo Miguel what it meant to be a Brachio Herder. 'I'm glad you asked, young man,' he replied. 'My grandson tends not to want to know about such things.'

Javier bristled at this, but listened politely. A Brachio Herder's job, Poppo Miguel explained, wasn't just to keep the brachios from entering the villages; it was also to keep the villagers from entering the jungle. The idea was to keep them apart, so each could live peacefully in their own world.

'Here in Mexico we have the purest breed of Yucatan Brachios, which are the wildest and the hardest to tame. Your punk was probably reared in captivity.' Poppo Miguel gestured towards where Budge could be heard munching away on the vegetation. 'Normally they live in dense jungles in Mexico and beyond, but occasionally they stray out of the jungle and wreak all sorts of havoc in the villages, plantations and farmlands surrounding it. The fields of tasty plants are too tempting for them. Most of it gets trampled, which naturally causes grief for many people. To try to prevent this there have always been Brachio Herders who have passed down, from generation to generation, the secrets of how to tame and ride wild brachiosaurs. I used to slowly track the many wild herds through the jungle from a distance. When they got too close to civilisation I would be there to help deter the herds from getting too close and into trouble. I used to receive donations of food and lodging in return from the thankful people. Sadly this task is now performed by men who patrol the jungle with guns.' Poppo Miguel sighed deeply. 'Alas, when I lost my son, that chain was broken. For a long time I have been the last of my kind.'

It was a sobering topic, and they ate in relative silence until the old man pressed on. 'Beatrice said you were looking for a Saurman temple,' he said, 'but Theodore says you're looking for a lost city. What are you actually here to do?'

Bea and Theodore both looked at each other, expecting the other to say something, but neither spoke. Bea hoped Theodore would take the lead, but clearly he hadn't decided how much to reveal.

'Tell me in your own time,' Poppo Miguel said at last, breaking the awkward silence.

♦ ♦ ♦

At dawn Bea took the opportunity to open her sketchbook and draw Carter and Buster all cuddled up with Budge, fast asleep. Javier was the next to wake up and sat beside her, watching as her hand flew over the page making pencil marks, and then as she filled the scene in with her watercolours. He whistled at the finished result. 'Very fine,' he remarked. 'You must have had a lot of practice.'

'My grandmother, Bunty, always encouraged me to draw; she said I had to record my travels and all the amazing things I saw. She always said that I must have got this from my mother, as she was a wonderful artist.'

'You must miss them,' Javier said.

'Awfully,' Bea replied. 'Which is why I carry this with me.' Bea pulled from her old satchel her mother's large sketchbook. 'We found some of my parents' belongings in Aru,' she explained. 'They left a trunk behind before heading into the jungle.' She opened up the cover. 'I never knew what talent she really had until I saw this.'

Javier paid close attention as Bea flipped through the pages. They were filled with everything from small life studies of everyday objects to wildlife sketches and landscapes. There was even a drawing of baby Carter sleeping.

Bea turned the next page and turned it round so that Javier could get a closer look. 'Oh my goodness!' she gasped and stared at the abstract illustration in disbelief.

'What is it, Bea?' asked Javier.

She whistled. 'It's the map,' she said. 'Look – my mother drew another picture of it, but hers is sideways and with child-like expression!' She twisted the sketchbook back and forth. The thing that had been niggling at her mind, the feeling that she'd seen it before, was suddenly clear.

Bea's excited tones had woken Theodore, who came over to see what was going on. Sure enough in Grace's large sketchbook was a duplicate of the map complete with both sides and the same circles.

'Could they be pinpointing the location of the lost city, like a target?' Bea questioned aloud.

'Those roads and towns look out of place,' said Javier,

pointing to the map and the many lines that connected the dots that marked out familiar roads joining the towns he knew well. 'Hang on, this map is different. They're not roads. It's a symbol, the star constellation of Gemini.'

Bea looked closer. 'Are you sure?'

'That's Castor and that's Pollux, the twins.' Javier nodded. 'They hold hands and that star is at the centre of the constellation and circles. It has to be where the city is!'

'My goodness, you're right! Clever old Gracie.' Theodore smiled. 'All this time we've been looking in Franklin's journals, when Grace had the answer all along in her sketchbook!'

Carter and Lucia joined them as they marvelled at Bea's discovery.

'The handprints look the same as the markings I saw in America with Uncle Cash, and the ones the Steggi children placed on their stegs in Kenya,' Carter pointed out.

'It's all adding up together now. Mother filled it in with watercolour,' Bea realised. 'I didn't see the connection between it and the other map we made a rubbing of.' Bea pulled out the copy she had made from Franklin's journal. Side by side the two images looked to be completely different. Grace's was filled with details and exquisite hues, while Bea's rubbing was a crude negative produced by the dark graphite of a pencil. She placed her map over half of Grace's; it fitted perfectly.

14

A Happy Place

~ kiss goodnight ~

A crash up ahead made everyone stop in their tracks. Javier signalled for all to hang back as he cautiously went on to see what it could be. He came running back alarmed. 'It's a titanosaur devouring a couple of Irritants – hide!'

'We can't stay here,' said Theodore. 'We're downwind.'

Budge stomped anxiously.

'It'll sniff out this punk brachio in no time,' said Poppo Miguel, who was mounted upon him, clinging on tight, and attempted to turn him round, but Budge was young and ill-trained, and, living up to his name, he refused to move.

'Budge, Budge!' Bea ordered from below impatiently, but instead of moving along he let out a joyful honk, thinking that Bea wanted to play.

The sound was enough to cause the titanosaur to pause its meal and look up. Poppo Miguel was right; it couldn't resist the whiff of a larger meal nearby, and started moving towards them, pushing trees aside violently as it approached.

'Quick!' Javier shouted. 'Climb as high as you can!' In a panic he, Theodore and Bea started to scale the nearest trees. Poppo Miguel and Lucia remained on Budge. Bea immediately got a foothold on a branch and began to inch her way further upwards, propelled by sheer adrenaline.

Carter, perched high atop Buster, was curious to see the saur everyone feared, and decided to face it head on. Theodore shouted after him, but it was no use. Carter's fearless nature was not shared by the saur he was riding. Buster grew trepidatious, moving his big head from side to side, and took a few steps backwards.

Its face filled with blood, making its head turn red in a matter of moments. Even its light pink eyes seemed to darken as it looked around at the frightened group and great globs of saliva dribbled from its lips. Lucia stifled a scream.

Carter did what he always did when coming across a saur new to him; he stared at it with an intense curiosity. The titanosaur had a similar body shape to the other tyrants he had seen, but there was a lot that was different. For starters, it was probably more closely related to an allosaur, as it had three fingers, not two. Then there were the long extended spines that created a raised ridge all down its back. When it roared it shook its head from side to side, sending a ripple waving down them to the tip of its heavyset tail. Its extended spines and bulk made it appear a lot bigger than the biggest tyrant he had met, the

White Titan Tyrant in Kenya, which was lean and agile in comparison. This was heavier all round, and it only had short feathers on its ankles. The rest of its body was covered in hard-looking thick scaly skin that seemed to pulse between tones of dark green and red.

The monstrous saur shook out a second roar, then moved boldly towards them, looking ready to pounce. Then one of its blood-red eyes was caught by something, and it stopped. At exactly its eye level Bea was perched upon a branch and staring in fear right back at it. Everyone gasped as it took a closer look and dwarfed her with its huge head. Bea clung on for dear life, knowing that the next moment might be her last. She closed her eyes tight and with one free hand instinctively grasped both the locket that housed her parents' photos and the twin's opalised keystone.

When she was desperate, sad or lonely the comfort that her parents, or at least a very small reminder of them, were sealed in the silver locket, would always bring Bea back to a happy place. Now, her mind racing, she recalled the morning in Aru when she had discovered that the locket was gone. When she'd first seen Carter's blue eyes staring back at her from high above in a tree. Bunty, her dear grandmother, smelling of roses, insisting the locket had been taken by rats, or something scavenging around the camp . . . but it wasn't. It suddenly occurred to her that it was the first time all four of them – Franklin, Grace,

Bea and Carter – had been together in one place. In spirit, at least. She remembered how Carter had suddenly dropped down under the strange rainbow tree amongst his clan of shadow raptors, and presented himself to his remaining family, unaware of who they were. She recalled running from gunshots and that horrid man Christian Hayter – and finding the Long-Tailed Raptor of Paradise and being rescued by the strange Saurman, Kunava, who had returned her locket to her.

Breathing steadily, she forced herself to call to mind more happy memories: photographs; a trunk full of treasured belongings; the way her beloved grandmother Bunty held her umbrella over her arm; her mother's sketchbook, so like her own; a music box that, when wound up, played a lovely tune. Although she'd been so young when her parents left, she could somehow hear her mother's gentle voice singing her to sleep – the same lullaby every night, which echoed the music box's melody. It became so real she could hear it – a string of notes floating in the air about her in the tree – and without even knowing she was doing it she began to sing along.

> *Glitterbone, sparklestone*
> *Twice-birthed child*
> *In a saur's nest you must hide*
> *From there will a Saurman rise*

Glitterbone, sparklestone
Twin-starred morn
One life lived but two lives long
Order of the Saurmen born

Time seemed to stop as Bea's voice lifted clear and strong. Everyone could hear her, but no one dared make a sound. Transported by her memories, Bea held out her hand to touch her mother's face as it bent over her. In her mind Bea could see her mother as clear as day leaning in to kiss her goodnight, and she smiled.

Glitterbone, sparklestone
Double-yolk egg
By a saur you once were fed
To the temple you'll be led

Glitterbone, sparklestone
Split-seamed son
A tree you'll find, but only one
When you're called, you must come

Glitterbone, sparklestone
Two-times strong
Know what's right, do no wrong
Pass along this sacred song

As the lullaby receded Bea slowly returned to herself, opening her eyes to discover, to her utter astonishment, that she had just kissed a titanosaur on the nose. She was caressing its scaly pink muzzle as it sniffed her out. To everyone's shock, the creature lowered its head, which had returned to being pale pink, took a step back, and turned round, treading softly back into the jungle from where it came.

'How on earth did you do that?' Theodore asked, catching her in his arms as she descended.

'I don't know,' she replied in a daze. 'It was the strangest thing: I was in a different place, somewhere between my memories and my dreams, and it seemed as if everything just slowed down. Everything became calm and focused. I'm not exactly sure how to explain it.'

'I've been there too, Bea,' Theodore told her. 'It's real. You've connected with your keystone and it connected you to that titanosaur. Like your brother, you were able to pacify it.' Theodore hugged his god-daughter tightly.

Javier explained to his grandfather what had transpired, but Poppo Miguel seemed to already know. Lucia kept shaking her head in disbelief that they were all still alive. Carter hugged his sister with pride. Their lives had been turned upside down and changed beyond belief in the short amount of time since they had found each other! Bea felt she now had a greater insight into how fearlessly Carter saw the world and how he befriended the saurs around him.

◆ ◆ ◆

The titanosaur had returned to its lunch and continued to ignore the humans as they tentatively pushed forward. There wasn't much left of the Irritators now. As the humans disappeared into the jungle the titanosaur coughed up a chunk of Irritator. It had gorged itself to the point that nothing else would fit inside its stomach. It sniffed the lump of regurgitated saur, and then raised its head high

and inhaled deeply. The air was wet and filled with pollen, insects and scent from everything within a mile. There was nothing to challenge his right to his kill, but there were a multitude of smaller creatures that could strip the remaining flesh from the two Irritators in less than a day, so it had to be made secure. It took a while to get a leg from both saurs in its mouth but as soon as it did the titanosaur dragged the remaining feast back to its nesting site for the next day.

Within an hour the jungle returned to its noisy self, as everything that had stood quietly in fear went back to its daily business. Animals and insects set about clearing up the remnants of the Irritators and squabbled with each other for the best bits.

It was then that Ash and Bishop dropped down into the blood-stained undergrowth from the trees in which they had been hiding.

'I thought that titanosaur was never going to leave,' said Ash, relieving himself behind a tree.

Bishop paced around, making sure the coast was clear. 'What should we do – go back or follow them?'

Ash wiped his sweating brow. 'Both,' he said, pointing back in the direction from which they had come. 'You go and tell the boss we have them, and to bring us some more saurs to ride.' He looked at the trampled undergrowth left by the punk brachio. 'I'll keep tabs on them.'

'You all right on your own?' Bishop asked.

Ash shrugged. 'Are any of us?'

Bishop nodded. 'We were lucky they showed up.' He laughed nervously. 'I thought we were going to be dessert for a while back there.'

'Going toe to toe with a titanosaur on our own was perhaps a bit foolhardy,' Ash said.

Bishop raised his eyebrows. 'However much the boss hates them,' he admitted, 'we owe those kids our lives.'

15

A New Perspective

~ the opal eyeball ~

They walked on, taking turns riding on Budge with Poppo Miguel and Buster, who was getting used to friends of Carter and Bea riding him. Theodore walked ahead checking for signs of the Rebels and making sure there were no more titanosaurs to surprise them. Poppo Miguel took the opportunity to have a chat with Carter when it was their turn together. 'Tell me about yourself,' he asked, and Carter began relaying his story – partly his own experience, and partly what others had told him about his origins. Poppo Miguel listened intently. When a low-hanging vine threatened to swing into the old man's face, Carter moved to catch it, but Poppo Miguel ducked just in time.

'How did you know?' Carter asked.

'I could see it,' Poppo Miguel answered.

'But your eyes – they don't work!'

'True. But I have noticed that when Theodore and Beatrice are nearby, it's as if I can see a little. And when you're nearby I find I can see quite a lot.'

'How can that be?' asked Carter.

'I do not know,' Poppo Miguel replied. 'My eyes, they used to be blue, like yours.'

'You know what colour my eyes are?'

'Yes,' Poppo Miguel said. 'But what I see *behind* your eyes is more important.'

'What do you mean?'

'I see the truth. This is what you must see also. Tell me again how your parents met their fate?'

Carter reiterated that they had been attacked and killed by shadow raptors.

Poppo Miguel stopped and shook his head. 'No,' he said. 'This is what you have been told, not what you see. Look again.'

'What am I supposed to see?' Carter asked, bewildered.

'I see a man with one hand, protecting them.'

Kunava! Carter swallowed hard. There was no possible way that Poppo Miguel could have known about Kunava in Aru, on the other side of the world. He sensed both profound discomfort and yet great peace. It was a confusing sensation. Suddenly he had an idea. Carter reached into his satchel, withdrew his tin of precious objects, and from it the opal eyeball he'd been secretly carrying around for a while.

'I have something to help you see,' he told Poppo Miguel, and carefully put it into his palm.

A glorious smile lit upon the old man's wrinkled

face. 'Thank you, my boy,' he said, emotion choking his gentle voice. 'I know what this is and it being a gift makes it all the more powerful.'

Carter had always left his sister and Theodore to discuss in detail the nature of the power these strange stones had. He knew they were important, especially to Saurmen, but for Carter, who did not need a keystone to connect with saurs, they were mostly unimportant. Now he realised that Bea and Theodore had got so bogged down in the 'how and why' of the mysterious opals that they could not see what was obvious to him: keystones helped bring the secretive Saurmen together. It was becoming increasingly clear to Carter that Poppo Miguel was more than just a Brachio Herder.

✦ ✦ ✦

They were starting to ascend into the hills, which could be seen at a distance from the town. Bea consulted her map, and checked it against the one Lambert had given them. The path they followed appeared

to be a series of switchbacks, and after a while a different set of sounds replaced those they'd grown used to and the foliage changed. The chatter of creatures that swung through the trees seemed to gossip about the strangers in their midst, and an occasional howl reverberated across the hollow spaces to remind them that large predators also called this place home.

As they approached the summit they stopped at a small clearing that afforded them a spectacular view of the land below. 'I'm sure it's here somewhere,' Bea kept on saying, checking their location for features she could see both on her map and as she looked around her.

They could see the town a long way off, and at intervals breaking the thick jungle canopy a series of clear circular spaces.

'What are those?' Carter asked.

'Looks like it could be illegal logging,' Theodore suggested, and located where it was on his map.

Lucia came over and confirmed what he thought. 'It's the avocado plantation where I used to work,' she said.

'It's also in the red area, where the Rebels are supposed to be camped out,' Theodore added.

'From here I can see more clearings than those I worked on,' Lucia noted. 'It looks like quite an operation.'

Bea came over to take a look and get her bearings again before looking intently at her mother's map. 'It must be here,' she muttered. She sat down next to Poppo Miguel, who was resting. 'I don't see any evidence of a city up here,' she confided. 'I think the ancient people who made the original map my mother copied obviously embellished it a bit. Look, here is this huge tree just past the city with these strange flowers, or blobs, under it. We haven't seen anything like that in the jungle so far.'

'A temple tree,' said Poppo Miguel to Bea's surprise. 'That is a sacred place.'

'Do you see it too, Poppo Miguel? Have you been there? Is that where you grew up?' asked Bea.

'I grew up a very long time ago,' Poppo Miguel replied. 'Things were different then. The temple tree is a place where all my family have been, including Javier briefly when he was a baby, when his mother remained at home recuperating from his birth.' Even though he said it very quietly, everyone heard.

'What did you call it?' asked Theodore.

'It is a sacred Saurman temple tree.'

Theodore's eyes widened. Bea was staring at the old man open-mouthed. Only Carter appeared to take the information calmly.

'How do you know this?' Theodore asked.

Poppo Miguel smiled. Now was the right time to explain. 'Because I am a Brachio Saurman,' he said proudly.

'A Brachio *Herder*, you mean,' said Lucia, shaking her head. 'Come on, let's get you into the shade, old man – the sun has been cooking your brains.'

Carter spoke up, placing a hand on Poppo Miguel's shoulder. 'Tell them.'

'Tell us what?' Bea and Theodore asked at the same time.

'It was the local villagers who gave us the name Brachio Herders,' Poppo Miguel explained, 'but before that my people were simply called Saurmen. My job was not just to keep the brachios from exiting the forest; it was also to keep the people from coming into it and finding the temple and the city.'

Javier rolled his eyes.

'Many young people don't believe that Saurmen existed,' Poppo Miguel said.

'Like *el Ratón de los Dientes*,' Javier groaned.

'What's that?' Carter asked.

'The Tooth Mouse,' Javier translated. 'When you lose a tooth you put it under your pillow at night. The Tooth Mouse comes and exchanges it for a gift.'

'We have the Tooth Fairy,' Bea said. 'She does the same thing!'

'Some things are meant to disappear into history,' Poppo Miguel continued. 'If there are no Saurmen left in the world, then they might as well live in myth. Like *el Ratón de los Dientes*,' he added pointedly.

'So you're protecting the Saurman temple and the lost city from the outside world?' Theodore clarified. 'Only you know where the temple is located?'

'Correct,' said Poppo Miguel.

Javier stopped poking the ground with a stick and sat up. He looked at his grandfather as if he'd never seen him before.

'The temple is not in the same place as the city?' asked Theodore, scratching his head.

'No. I do not know where the city is,' Poppo Miguel said. 'The two places are very different. To discover the lost city you need a map; the temple can only be found if you are a true Saurman. You know this. The keystones you carry –' he pointed to Bea and Theodore – 'they will lead you only to the temple.'

Theodore hung his head and nodded. 'Yes, I seem to have a knack for finding things that can't be found,' he replied. 'It appears to be a Saurman thing I can do quite well.'

'But we do have the map!' Bea said excitedly. 'We can find both places!'

'The original map was made a very long time ago,' Poppo Miguel reminded her. 'You were right that the jungle used to be bigger back then, but you have overlooked something more important.'

Bea was hanging on the old man's every word. 'Go on.'

'The city – it was reclaimed by the jungle a very long time ago. No one has found it, though many have tried. It truly does seem lost.'

'Oh.' Bea was deflated. She kicked herself for thinking that an entire city could simply exist unbeknownst to the people who had lived here for generations.

'You keep saying you have to find the lost city like it's something your friend Lambert ordered you to do, but what if the Saurmen intend it not be found?' Poppo Miguel asked.

'You think the Saurmen wanted the city to fade away?'

'Yes,' Poppo Miguel continued. 'If this place is uncovered, it will be destroyed by those who wish to see it. This place is for the plants, the animals – not for people. The last time people tried to settle here it ended badly.'

'What people?' Theodore asked.

'The people who once lived in the city you have been told to find. Their civilisation was lost – it failed.'

Theodore sighed. 'Gosh, I never thought of it like that.'

Carter and Bea understood that Poppo Miguel had his reasons for not wanting to find the lost city, and they made sense.

'But it feels like we're meant to be the ones to rediscover it,' Bea said, looking around and then back at the map. 'We're exactly where the city should be.'

'You're right, Poppo,' said Theodore. 'It's gone now, fallen back into the ground. There is no longer anything to see up here; whatever was once here has been utterly consumed by the jungle.' Theodore patted his knife and the keystone set in the end of its handle and got up. 'I guess we should head off and find the Saurman temple instead.'

Poppo Miguel nodded. 'There is much more you will learn from that place.'

Bea wanted to ask Poppo Miguel hundreds of questions, but realised she would have to wait. Javier and Lucia helped him get back on top of Budge and chatted away, asking him why he had kept so much from them. As Carter readied Buster, Theodore hung back. He could see that Bea was deflated.

'I know you wanted to find the lost city, Bea, because that was what your father's journal mentioned, and it feels like we're giving up on it. But remember: it was you who found the inscription of the twins' journey at the saur graveyard; it was you who found half the map in your father's journal. You found the full map in your mother's sketchbook and you led us all here to where the city used to be.' He winked at her. 'You did all this on your own, and I know Franklin and Grace would have been ever so proud of you for trying to finish off what they started all those years ago. And now we have a Saurman sacred temple to explore instead!'

'But I also wanted to prove to Lambert I could do it,' Bea groaned, bending down and picking up a solitary rock that had some moss growing on it, 'and all I have to show him is this worthless rock.'

All of a sudden, from up ahead, there were cries, and then a thundering sound of falling rocks shaking the ground.

Carter raced past Bea and Theodore on Buster and skidded to an abrupt stop. A deep hole had opened up in the ground. Budge's long neck and head emerged and glanced around with a bewildered look on his face.

15

What is Going On?

~ putting out small fires ~

The patrol leader paused and held up his arm to signal silence. The perimeter had been peaceful all night – no titanosaurs to threaten the sleeping brachios at any rate. But now he could hear something approaching through the undergrowth. He crouched and readied his gun, and the rest followed his lead. 'Who goes there?' he called out, as much a warning as a question.

A man emerged in the darkness, and, stumbling, fell into the clearing. 'Don't shoot!' he gasped, his arms held high despite his obvious exhaustion.

The patrol dragged him away from the undergrowth and poured a flask of water on his face, causing the man to splutter and cough.

'Bishop,' the man wheezed, 'I'm Bishop. Mr Hayter's man.'

'What were you doing in the jungle?' the patrol leader demanded. 'No one leaves this camp unless General Vulpez says so.'

'Following orders,' Bishop gasped, sitting up. 'Ash and

I were sent to track some people.'

'We were not told of this. Where is your friend now?' the patrol leader snapped.

'We were attacked by a titanosaur,' Bishop explained. 'We climbed a tree just in time. Ash followed the people we were tracking.' He stood up shakily and brushed himself down. 'I need to inform my boss of these developments.'

The patrol leader lowered his gun. 'And I need to inform the General. Let's see what he has to say about this first,' he said gruffly.

♦ ♦ ♦

General Vulpez stormed into the hatchery to confront the Doctor, who'd been inspecting the eggs. 'We need to talk, NOW!' he shouted, and stomped his foot.

The Doctor met the General's angry stare and calmly asked his assistant to leave. 'And how can I help you?' he asked coolly.

'What is going on here?' the General demanded. 'I thought this operation was self-contained. We were to clear the jungle and breed these saurs –' he swept his hand to indicate the rows and rows of eggs nestled in their nest – 'in order to supply the Sauria Trading Company with quality meat.'

The Doctor nodded calmly. 'And that is exactly what we are doing, General,' he replied.

Before General Vulpez could speak again, the door swung open, sending in a shaft of hot daylight and

Christian Hayter, who was pushed inside by two armed guards. 'This'd better be important,' Hayter grumbled.

'It is. I have just been told that Señor Logan, that English man I intercepted at the mayor's office, and who knew way too much about this place, is now traipsing around the jungle nearby, and by all accounts he is with the same locals we suspected of talking about what happens here. We tried to silence them by burning down their house, but obviously it has been unsuccessful.' The General glared at Hayter. 'And Señor Bishop has informed me that your other idiot is still out there following them. What business are they of yours? Why did you send your men after them?"

Hayter thought quickly. 'I ordered my men to track them to make sure they don't stumble across us.'

'Interesting.' General Vulpez paused for dramatic effect. 'Señor Bishop mentioned something about them looking for the fabled lost city.'

Hayter and the Doctor looked at each other.

'This is news to us,' Hayter fibbed. 'I thought that place was a myth.'

'It is,' General Vulpez cut him off quickly. 'Unless Señor Logan and his sympathisers know something I don't.'

'Your concern is unfounded,' the Doctor said patiently. 'We are all on the same side here.' He adjusted his dark glasses. 'Trust me, the Viscount does not care for these people or this city – just our business here raising tritops. As you say, this city does not exist. Nothing remains of the Mayan or Aztec Empires except some crumbling monuments. There is nothing of value in this jungle except the land we're reclaiming for you.'

'Logan must know something about the lost city,

otherwise why dare come into this jungle,' the General responded irritably. 'The locals are scared of us.'

'Don't worry about them – or the locals who help them,' the Doctor added. 'Chances are slim to none they will leave this jungle alive. Our man Ash will take care of that – you've witnessed his abilities.'

'But I *do* worry about people wandering around in my jungle,' General Vulpez snapped. 'I cannot have this operation exposed. It is key to my success here.'

'Let's leave Ash to watch over them and wait until the Viscount returns before you do anything hasty,' the Doctor advised, trying to calm the situation.

The General paused to consider and lit a cigar, causing the Doctor to wince. 'Please, General – no smoking in the hatchery. There are lots of combustibles in here.'

The General spat on the floor instead. 'This is MY country,' he growled. 'MY rules.'

'Even so,' the Doctor reiterated, standing his ground, 'it would be a great shame for all our hard work to go up in smoke.'

'It is *my* jungle, and I will not wait for the Viscount to return from the city!' the General shouted, enraged once more. 'You, Señor Hayter, will accompany me and my men to find these people and bring them back here to be locked up.'

'I take my orders from the Viscount,' replied Hayter.

'Unless you want to be locked up as well, you will do as

I command,' the General snarled. 'We head off now. Señor Bishop was not very good about hiding his tracks. It won't take long to catch up with them.'

General Vulpez brought the cigar up to his mouth, staring at the Doctor as he did so. Then, instead of drawing from it, the General flipped it round and extinguished it on his tongue with a sizzling sound, before kicking the door open and storming out, barking orders to the guards standing outside.

17

The Sinkhole

~ hidden treasure~

'Are you okay down there?' Theodore yelled. 'Is anyone hurt?'

Lucia's voice came up. 'I – I think Poppo's all right,' she called shakily, 'but Javier's hurt!'

'Quick!' cried Bea. 'Theodore, get them out of there!'

'Help me rig up a length of rope from these vines,' Theodore replied in a hurry, and Bea jumped up to join him. Carter was busy trying to calm Budge, who was understandably startled. The enormous young saur skittishly attempted to rear up in a vain attempt to climb out of the hole, but this just made the sides crumble, sending more rock and dirt onto Carter, Bea and Theodore. Carter calmly stroked Budge on the nose and, as he stopped struggling, he pointed him towards some juicy ferns that the punk could reach easily.

From below, Lucia confirmed that it appeared

Javier had broken his ankle. They could hear the boy crying and whimpering in pain. Theodore tossed one end of the vine rope down to her, and Carter tied the other end round Buster. Lucia strapped Javier's leg to Poppo Miguel's cane and looped the vine round his shoulders. Helping him to his feet, she steadied him as he held on tightly and watched as the others winched him gently up. Once clear of the hole, Theodore checked Javier over, and as soon as he saw his misshapen ankle he winced in sympathy.

'Hang in there,' Bea said, trying to comfort him.

'Bea, Carter – you'll need to go down to Poppo,' Theodore said. 'Javier needs Lucia up here with him.'

Lucia called up for the rope as Bea and Carter carefully climbed down the brachio's long neck and descended into the darkness to attend to Poppo Miguel. Theodore helped pull Lucia to the surface so she could tend to her son.

'It's bad,' he confirmed. 'We'll need to get him to a doctor as quickly as we can.'

'But we are days away from a doctor and we can't go into town!' Lucia cried wretchedly. 'The army – they will find us and then what?'

Theodore wanted to comfort her, but truthfully he was unsure he could. He pulled Lucia into a hug.

Down in the pit, Carter waited for his eyes to adjust to the darkness before he inspected Budge for any sign of injury. Bea felt her way round him towards Poppo Miguel. The air was a lot cooler, and it reminded Bea of being in the twins' presence in the saur graveyard, which sent a shiver down her spine. It also reminded her of the time she was imprisoned in the cave in Kenya with Micheal Keat and that horrid man Christian Hayter. She looked about, but it was hard to make out the space. When researching their trip Bea had read about the strange limestone sinkholes that peppered the Yucatan landscape like Swiss cheese – this must be one of them.

Poppo Miguel was sitting in a shaft of sunlight, resting against Budge's flank. He appeared to have slid down the animal's side for a relatively soft landing. He assured them both he was all right and in no hurry to get out back into the boiling hot day above. 'I think you may be right, Beatrice,' he said.

'Right about what?' she replied

'The lost city. Perhaps we were meant to find it after all.' He turned to face her. 'Everything happens for a reason, even falling in here.'

Bea looked back at him in amazement. 'Falling into a sinkhole?' she asked. 'I think it was just an unlucky accident.'

'Look again.' He smiled at her. 'Even I can see it's not a sinkhole. He tapped his foot on the ground. 'Beneath us is solid. If it was a sinkhole it would be filled with crystal-clear water. This was no accident.'

Bea spun round and studied their surroundings

again. It appeared that Poppo Miguel was right. The space was too symmetrical.

'Theo, you'd better get down here!' she called up to the surface.

Theodore shimmied down the brachio's neck into the hole. Once his eyes adjusted he let out a whistle. This was no ordinary sinkhole; this was a magnificently decorated chamber.

Bea lit one of the candles Carter had stashed in his satchel so they could look around.

The candle's glow illuminated a number of archways that let out onto other rooms of equal splendour. It was hard to make out what was man-made and what was natural, as what must have once been wide passages were now tight warrens of roots and fallen rocks. 'This must have been a palace at one time,' Bea said, 'but the jungle's taken over.'

'It's astonishing,' Theodore replied distractedly as he peered all about him, trying to assess where on earth they found themselves. 'We can't be down here long,' he cautioned, 'but we need to know what this is. Bea, make sure you take some photographs if you can. Carter, do you have some more candles?'

'No,' Carter said, 'just one – but it is long. We can cut it into three pieces and each have one.'

'Smart lad!' Theodore nodded approvingly and made quick work of the task.

Calling up to the surface, Theo established that Lucia and Javier were able to rest a while, and leaving Poppo Miguel to rest, the children and Theodore ventured into other rooms to explore. In the next room Bea looked up and saw, growing through cracks in the ceiling, the twisted roots of trees above, adding their own filigree to the rich patterns on the walls. Animals nesting in every available nook and cranny were startled by the light that illuminated a place that had been dark for hundreds, if not a thousand years.

'Careful as you go,' warned Theodore after he slipped

on a wet stone and stumbled. 'The ceiling and jungle above could fall in at any time!' He pushed his way through an opening into a dark chamber but was forced back by hundreds of startled ghats, which billowed out screeching, flapping up around Poppo Miguel and Budge before exiting into the daylight like a cloud of thick black smoke.

Bea pulled out the camera Micki Myers had given her and began to take photographs. She just hoped they would develop, as it was dark in there. Every now and then one of them let out an 'Oh!' or an 'Ah!', which reverberated or became muffled, depending on the space they were in, a bit like a hall of mirrors with sound instead of reflection.

Everywhere they looked the jungle had tried to reclaim what was once designed by man. Roots had cracked the paving stones underneath and twisted through, so that at first glance they appeared to be snakes. Through what were once skylights in carved roofs, vegetation hung in layers and loops, dripping moisture from tendrils fine as silk. The rock that produced the area's sinkholes was soft enough to easily hollow out using primitive tools, and the spaces these people had created took advantage of the caves and tunnels that had formed naturally underground. One room appeared to have once been a courtyard open to the sun, but now was covered with a roof of tangled roots, through which slim shafts of light filtered down, catching a multitude of insect wings.

Another looked like it had been a bath or pool, with a deep hollow cut into the floor and stone benches placed all around it.

Everywhere she turned Bea found something that caught her interest – a carved detail here, a plaited root there, the fragments of a painted wall, an exotic moth, the glint of some barely perceptible light hitting gold.

A carved face looked out from a small rock covered in moss. Bea brushed away the years of growth to reveal grooves and markings all over it. Carter came over with a similar decorative carved figurine in his hand.

'Look – they're different saurs,' said Carter. 'Yours seems to be a tritops and this must be a brachio.' They found a few more, placing them in their satchels to clean and inspect later.

At one point Bea let out a surprised yelp as she backed into Carter. He was busy conducting his own survey and was marvelling at several beetles that looked tasty. 'Mother and Father would have loved to see this place,' Bea said. It's incredible, isn't it? This must have been what it was like for Howard Carter – your namesake – when he discovered those famous tombs in Egypt.'

Carter hadn't really considered the importance of his name before and beamed with pride in the dark.

'Some of these designs seem familiar from Mother's sketchbook,' Bea said, inspecting a wall filled with figures.

Carter took a closer look. 'I've seen something like

this on a wall close to where I found the Great Zino with Uncle Cash and Wolf,' he remarked. 'Same handprints.' He placed his hand onto the wall where someone a very long time ago had done the same. 'Also looks like Sholo and Sheia's stegs – they had handprints, too.'

'These carvings are similar to the ones in the twins' temple,' Theodore remarked, coming closer, 'though perhaps the ones we saw in the saur graveyard were a bit cruder. Perhaps made by less skilled people.'

The way to one chamber was barred by glistening spikes of stalactites, formed over the centuries by the accumulation of minerals in rainwater that dripped constantly from the ceiling. Below them, a mirror image had formed of stalagmites growing upwards. They had not quite met, and appeared in the candles' glow forbiddingly like Buster's gaping jaws. Carter watched as a drop of water formed and trembled at the end of one of the long teeth, before dropping directly onto the tooth below.

'I don't think we're going to be able to get in there,' Bea remarked.

Carter touched his finger to the tip of one of the spikes to catch a drop of water, just as Bea snapped a photograph of him doing so. Startled by the flash, Carter jumped forward. There was a loud SNAP as the stalactite broke and crashed to the ground.

Carter found himself wedged between the stony

teeth. As he tried to free himself, he glanced through to the next cave. Perhaps the way wasn't barred after all. Carter gently lifted his other arm and shoulder through the gap he'd created, and then his legs, snapping off a few more spikes as he went. 'Bea . . .' he said.

'Right behind you,' she answered.

They stepped into a ghostly space that felt like being directly under the night sky, though they were far underground. But the twinkles weren't stars. 'Gosh,' Bea exclaimed as she examined the walls more closely. They were panelled with obsidian and black opal.

'Keystone!' Carter uttered in a hushed voice.

Bea turned round and adjusted her camera to try to capture a shot of the walls when something caught her eye through the viewfinder. She pulled the camera away and sucked in her breath. She shivered involuntarily as it occurred to her that she was the first person to set eyes on the hidden treasure before her. She could imagine historians the world over poring over it and it being put on display in a grand museum, where visitors would be prevented from getting too close by a glass case and velvet rope. Yet here she was, and for the moment it was all her own.

18

The Lost City

~ the Secret Order of Saurmen ~

'Theo!' Bea yelled. 'You have GOT to see this!'

Theodore clambered through the opening, breaking off a bit more of it as he did so. 'What on earth is the matter?' he mumbled as he pulled at his trousers, which had become snagged on one of the stalagmites. He joined Carter and Bea, and looked up. Before them sat a magnificent object on a plinth of solid rock – a huge titanosaur skull, completely inlaid with gold and gemstones, which even in the dim light gave off a dazzling aura. It spoke of unimaginable wealth.

His jaw dropped. 'What is that?' he gasped as Bea and Carter illuminated the skull with their candles.

Carter peered deeply at the black opals that were set into the eye sockets. Each one was as big as a tennis ball. He had never seen anything like this in his short experience as a human being. He had occasionally played with pebbles and old bones, but even the keystones that Theodore and Bea prized had never held his interest long. However, the people who had once lived here had taken the carving of these stones to extraordinary lengths. The skull was both harrowing and beautiful at the same time.

'What are we going to do with it?' Bea asked. 'If we leave it here, the stalactites will consume it and it will be lost.'

'More to the point,' Theodore ventured, 'now that we've let the light in, this place will be found soon enough by others. What if the Rebels get to it? I suggest we take the skull so that it doesn't fall into the wrong hands. Lambert has the kind of connections who can make sure it is taken care of.'

'Are you sure we should move it?' Carter asked, his voice uneasy. 'Can we carry it? What if –'

'We'll make it work – don't worry,' Theodore interrupted. 'But we've got to act quickly; Javier's waiting for us up above.'

Carter shrugged. To him one object was as good as another, and some were infinitely more valuable. A candle, for instance, was far more useful to carry around than this giant lump of metal and stone. But people were funny, and he was still figuring them out.

'Do you think Lambert knew this was here?' Bea asked as they lifted it carefully from its plinth. It was very heavy.

'I can't imagine how he'd anticipate this,' Theodore replied. 'Though it would certainly explain his willingness to foot the bill for this venture and why he was so keen for us to find this place. This skull adds considerable lustre to having his name associated with discovering the lost city.'

'I can't imagine what his wife Anya will think,' Bea added. 'She'd go bonkers for the chance to pose next to this

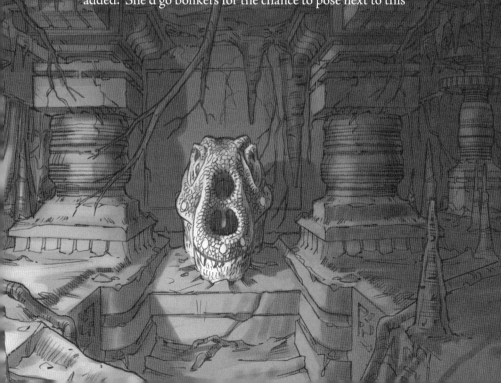

in all the magazines!'

One step at a time the three of them got themselves and the skull through the hole they'd made getting into the chamber, and carried it back to Poppo Miguel and Budge, who were waiting patiently.

'If only you could see what we've found,' Theodore said to Poppo Miguel as they set the skull down carefully.

'I have a good idea,' he answered enigmatically.

Something else occurred to Bea. 'Your keystone, did it lead us here, Theo?'

But Theodore shook his head. 'I didn't find this place – it was your map that led us here and Budge simply trod on the right spot.' He felt the end of his knife where his stone was set into it. 'It's cold, I feel nothing. This place means nothing to me.'

Poppo Miguel nodded. 'You're catching on,' he said. 'Keystones allow Saurmen to see their temples and find each other, no matter how widely they are scattered.'

'Which explains a lot,' Theodore muttered. 'Like how I found you.'

'Or rather how I was able to find you,' Poppo Miguel suggested with a grin. 'It works both ways.'

'But didn't you say that Saurmen once lived in this city?' Carter asked, confused. Until now the search for temples had been something he had left to Bea and Theodore, but now his curiosity had been awoken. 'There is so much opal in these walls.'

'The majority of the people who lived in this city were not Saurmen – far from it,' Poppo Miguel revealed.

'But if they were not Saurmen, then why the temple, and why all this?' Theodore wondered aloud.

But Bea was catching on faster than Theodore. 'I was under the impression the Saurmen were simple people, not given to displays of riches.'

'You're right,' Poppo Miguel said. 'Saurmen used to live here. Back before time began they first discovered this strange place and that the land here is full of opal.'

'Paradise Bird,' Bea butted in.

'Yes, that's what the Mayans called them. Some of these special opals had strange properties and they called them keystones.'

'They're actually the remains of dinosaurs,' said Theodore, who also wanted to show Poppo he knew what he was talking about.

'Problems happened when other people arrived,' Poppo Miguel went on. 'Traders told of a place with these glittering stones and men came who wanted to exploit the land.'

'Like the Gold Rush in California,' said Carter, thinking of his friend Wolf Cub and Uncle Cash.

Poppo Miguel nodded. 'Good – I'm glad you're all following me and know something of the Saurmen. Over time a city grew up around the Saurmen, but eventually they packed up and left, as the rulers no longer heeded their advice and became corrupt, valuing riches like this skull instead of human and saur lives. Without the Saurmen's wisdom, the civilisation fell apart, and soon it was reclaimed by the jungle. The Saurmen eventually returned long after it was abandoned and created a more fitting temple close by. Your map, Beatrice, must be a copy of the same one they used to return here.'

'How do you know this?' asked Bea.

'My father told me, and his father told him, and so on. We are not just Saurmen, Carter and Theodore – we are all part of the Secret Order of Saurmen. That's why it's sad that we are dying out, just like my profession as a Brachio Herder. The links are fragile and breaking.' Poppo Miguel sighed. The old man seemed overcome with emotion. 'When my son died, the family's keystone and brachio were lost. Javier, sadly, does not see the importance of old traditions and he doesn't want to risk the same fate as his father. But perhaps there is hope.'

Theodore was moved by the old man's speech but knew he could linger no longer if they were to escape the sinkhole. He clambered up to help Lucia prepare Buster to haul Poppo Miguel out, and to check on Javier's condition. Bea, meanwhile, asked Poppo Miguel to tell them more of what the Brachio Herdsman knew about the Saurmen.

'The ancient people,' Poppo Miguel explained to Bea and Carter, 'understood the bond between humans and saurs, and developed a relationship to the benefit of both. The humans relied on saurs to clear vegetation so that villages, towns and even cities could take hold. In return, the humans protected the saurs from predators, and reserved vast areas where they could roam free. A group of individuals called Saurmen developed the ability and found a way to communicate with the saurs. It starts at birth,' he told them, 'and after being placed in their nests as infants; Saurmen live for an extraordinarily long time, just like I have.' He paused. 'But unlike them I did not become the wise man of my community. But I won't be passing down my wisdom as it has done from generation to generation.' He looked up to the sky above the hole they were in. 'My son was killed and Javier does not want this life.'

Poppo Miguel sighed and then continued. 'The kings all looked to the Saurmen for advice, and they were highly regarded. But over time things changed; kings worked the saurs more harshly and chipped away at their territory. They enslaved many saurs and people to dig deeper and mine more and more of the minerals.'

'Just like that awful Hassler De Bois taking the Steggi children and making them dig for diamonds in Kenya,' said Bea, nudging her brother.

'The Saurmen tried to maintain balance,' Poppo Miguel continued, 'but were ignored. Because they were being overworked, the saurs didn't perform as well, and the cities suffered. In this culture twins have always been revered, so when a pair of conjoined twins were born to one king in particular it was decreed that they must be sacrificed to Gemini in order to appease the gods. The Saurmen, however, saw this as a dreadful omen, and foiled the king by kidnapping the twins and spiriting them away through their newly founded secret order.'

Bea listened, her mouth agape. 'The twins at the saur graveyard!' she exclaimed breathlessly. 'Surely they are one and the same!'

'What do you mean?' the old man asked curiously. 'The twins are just a myth, a story lost in time.' He paused. 'The Secret Order of Saurmen is as real as I am, though. We have dedicated our lives to protecting the saurs and the temples they built around the world, which are hidden to keep others from exploiting them. A true Saurman understands the harmonious rhythms of the natural world, where the oldest and youngest species lived together as equals. We still celebrate the twins with the Gemini Festival, when pairs of saurs are paraded through the streets, but it is just an old tradition now, leftover from a different time.'

Bea lifted the keystone that hung round her neck. 'No – you're wrong about the twins being a myth, Poppo – we've found them!' she exclaimed. 'They do exist! Theodore and my father discovered them years ago at their final resting place – a strange canyon filled with the bones of thousands of saurs. I've seen them! In fact my keystone once belonged to one of them.' Bea smiled proudly. 'Its twin stone lies with my father, where he died with my mother on Aru.'

Poppo Miguel gasped in awe. 'You have met the twins,

Castor and Pollux.'

After Bea and Carter told Poppo Miguel everything they knew about the saur graveyard and the twins, Theodore climbed back down to tell them that Buster was rigged up and ready to haul Poppo Miguel and Budge to safety. They just had to get Poppo Miguel into position. Theodore was amazed to hear what the children had discovered about the Secret Order of Saurmen and the significance of the Gemini Festival. He tapped his pocket. 'I've got the tickets to that right here,' he said, smiling. 'Boy, do we have good news for Lambert!'

'Tell me,' Poppo Miguel said, leaning in closer to Theodore, 'have you heard of the prophecy?'

'A little,' Theodore replied.

Poppo Miguel leant in very close while Bea and Carter were out of earshot, pulling the skull into position. 'The Saurmen saved the conjoined twins because they believed them to be the incarnation of the prophecy,' Poppo Miguel told him gravely. 'A boy born half saur, who would bring balance back to their world. It turned out they were wrong.' He gestured at Carter. 'Carter tells me he was raised by Raptors of Paradise as one of their own; now he lives as a human with you. Does it not seem strange to you that the opals here are called Paradise Birds and that Carter doesn't need one – yet somehow he possess a greater ability than any of us? Tell me, do you know if he was a twin?' He leant forward expectantly.

Theodore explained kindly that they had it on good authority that Carter was not a twin, and that he wasn't half saur.

'His strange circumstance is just the result of cruel fate that saw his parents die tragically,' said Theodore. He paused. 'Franklin's journals did mention this prophecy several times, however, and each time he did so it was slightly different. Like most things passed down from generation to generation, sometimes things get lost or changed along the way. Like evolution, everything is constantly changing; some of the ancient dinosaurs died out, as we know, but some evolved into the saurs and birds around us today.'

Just then Lucia called down to say she had Buster all ready to pull Poppo Miguel out, and he was gently hauled up to his family.

Bea, Carter and Theodore struggled, but managed to tightly bind the ancient skull with vines that had fallen in with them and manoeuvre it into position. The rope was lowered when Poppo Miguel was safely at the surface, and again they watched as it ascended to the heavens. But after it had disappeared through the opening, the vine rope never came back down.

'Hey, up there!' Theodore called, but no reply came.

'Hello?' he called out again, but there was silence. Something came spinning down instead, a tiny object they couldn't make out until it landed at their feet.

It was a cigar stub.

19

Who Are You Calling Rebels?

~ pit of despair ~

'*Mucho gracias, caballeros,*' a voice sang down. 'You are true friends of Mexico!'

A figure silhouetted by the sunlight peeked over the edge and laughed at them.

'Javier! Lucia!' Theodore cried out. 'Are you okay up there? Is Poppo all right?'

'Ye–' Lucia began before being quickly stifled.

'Quiet,' the voice could be heard saying. Then, 'Don't worry, your friends are safe and sound, except the boy – he looks to be in pain. Oh dear.'

Theodore, Bea and Carter's blood ran cold.

'Congratulations are in order,' continued the man. 'It looks like you have discovered what many people have failed to find. Tell me – are there more skulls down there like this one we have up here? It's quite spectacular.'

'No!' Carter shouted angrily.

'I find that hard to believe,' the man said. 'That is why

some of my men will soon be arriving with excavating equipment.'

'You can't do that!' Bea shouted up. 'The city needs to be preserved – you'll ruin it! We need to protect it. We found it first.'

The man laughed. 'Yes, thank you for that. It's very fortunate you left such clear tracks for us to follow!'

Bea felt wretched and confused. It hadn't occurred to her that they might have been followed by anyone.

'Why would the Rebels be interested in following us?' Theodore yelled.

'Who are you calling rebels? You are the rebel scum.'

'What?' said Theodore, utterly confused. Lucia let out a wail, and there was a scuffle.

'Mama!' Javier cried weakly, before a thump sounded.

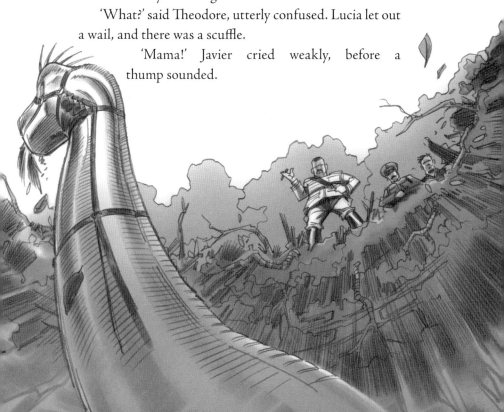

'There's no need to hit the boy!' Poppo Miguel cried.

'Hold her!' the voice commanded. 'Señora Cantera here and her family are known Rebel sympathisers who do not know when to keep their mouths shut. Luckily for you, someone very important wants you kept alive – for now.'

'I don't understand,' Theodore pressed. 'Who are you?'

'Why, Señor Logan – we have already met, don't you remember? I am General Vulpez.'

Theodore gulped and turned pale.

'Naturally I had you followed after our meeting,' the General said smugly. 'One cannot be too careful with all these Rebels about. Imagine my surprise when I discovered you were holed up with a former employee of the terribly suspicious avocado plantation you told me about! A hotbed of Rebel activity, no less! An astonishing turn of events, I'm sure you'll agree!'

Theodore's face coloured deeply in the dark. 'Lucia Cantera's no Rebel,' he cried hoarsely. 'You should be protecting good people like her, not blaming them!'

Bea could hear how mortified he was.

Lucia cried out again, and the General could be heard ordering someone to put a gag on her. 'I can see you didn't learn your lesson, troublemaker,' he growled. 'Your hair still smells of smoke. What – did your house burn down? No matter; I'll use you to make an example of to anyone else who thinks they can tell me what to do! Tie her up –

she's coming back with us.'

Suddenly the roof shuddered as something heavy rushed over it at speed, sending clods of earth raining down upon Theodore, Bea and Carter. Then there was the unmistakable sound of a Black Dwarf Tyrant's roar, followed by a blood-curdling yell, which was stopped short by the sound of gunfire and commotion.

Bea screamed.

'*Basta!*' the General shouted. 'Hold your fire!'

'Buster!' Carter cried out in a panic, and leapt forward to climb up Budge's neck.

Freshly alarmed at the shots being fired so close to his head, the punk brachio let out a distressed honk as Carter pulled himself onto his back, only for a torrent of rapid gunfire to rain down around him, causing Budge to writhe about yet more.

'Oh no you don't, boy,' General Vulpez warned. 'You'd better stay down there.' Bea pleaded for her brother to step back down but he clung on to Budge, desperately trying to calm him. 'Is my tyrant alive?' he called back up fearlessly, his voice cracking with terror. Thankfully he heard Buster emit the low rattling call he used to warn things away.

The General's voice could be heard saying, 'You're going to do what?' He returned to the opening shortly. 'Your tyrant is being confiscated,' he announced. 'My associate here wishes to retrain it.'

'No one can train a tyrant!' Theodore called. 'It's

suicide. Tell your associate he will be badly bitten as soon as he tries to approach. Only Carter can tame him.'

'Oh, only Carter, you say? Well, it looks like my friend has your tyrant under control. I am leaving half of my men here to ensure that you don't escape. It will be nightfall soon, so I will take my lovely new skull back with me. When I return you can show me around down there. Until we meet again, Rebels.' He could be heard laughing as he left.

'You can't take Buster!' Carter shouted after him.

But it was no good – within seconds all was silent up above.

'What's going on up there?' Theodore shouted, cupping his hands round his mouth to magnify his voice. 'What have you done with the Canteras and our tyrant?'

'Javier and I are still here,' Poppo Miguel shouted back. 'But they took Lucia!'

'Silence!' a guard shouted.

'What did the General mean when he said he had met you before?' Carter asked Theodore.

Bea glared at him in the dark.

Just when it seemed their predicament couldn't get any worse, the candle he was holding started to flicker wildly as it reached the liquid wax of the stump. Once night fell they'd be stuck underground in total darkness with a massive panicked saur.

Carter was distraught. He paced up and down, repeating Buster's name as if saying it enough would bring him back. Bea tried to reassure him, but nothing she said helped.

'What have I done?' Theodore groaned. 'I'm so, so sorry,' he said to Carter and Bea – and also to himself.

20

The Three *Abuelas*

~ the new temple tree ~

J avier grimaced as Poppo Miguel tended to his ankle as best he could under the close watch of the guards who had remained. 'My grandson needs a doctor,' he pleaded with them. 'His ankle is broken – he's in pain!'

'We have our orders, señor,' one of them barked.

Poppo Miguel tried a different tack. 'Why are you dressed like the Rebels and not in army uniform?'

The Rebel guard ignored him.

Javier groaned. He was drifting in and out of consciousness, and his ankle was very swollen, the skin now purple and stretched tight. He needed help.

'Señor, I need to relieve myself,' Poppo Miguel said. 'Let me step into the trees for a minute to do so.'

'Not a chance, old man,' the guard replied.

'Respectfully,' Poppo Miguel continued, 'I am blind; I could not possibly run away. Do not force an old man to soil himself. Let me have some dignity.'

The armed guard consulted his partner. 'Okay,' he said gruffly, 'but be quick about it!'

Poppo Miguel nodded his assent, and slowly got to his feet. Without his cane to guide him he stepped hesitantly towards the trees, holding out his arms as he went. He appeared frail, no longer like the man who had danced at a wedding just days before.

'I'll be right back,' Poppo Miguel whispered in Javier's ear in as reassuring a tone as he could muster. He crept on until the undergrowth concealed him.

After a few minutes had passed and Poppo Miguel had not come back, one of the guards called after him. 'Hey – old man! Time's up!'

There was no reply. Javier moaned.

'I said hurry up!' the guard called again. 'Don't make me come after you. I mean it!'

Still nothing.

'I warned you!' the guard said and stomped off into the trees. It became apparent, after hearing him call and get no reply, that he wasn't having any luck. 'Ramón!' the guard yelled back. 'Help me look for the old man!'

Another guard got to his feet reluctantly and went off to join in the search.

Javier stirred. 'Poppo?' he called out weakly, trying to raise himself on one elbow, then flinched from the pain of moving. 'Where did you go?' His voice grew desperate as he called out in anguish. 'Don't leave me!'

Soon, however, there was a swish of branches coming from the jungle, and voices. But the sounds grew louder

Something wasn't walking towards them – it was crashing. The guard who remained stepped back and forth, agitated. 'José?' he called out, 'Ramón?'

He was cut off by a deafening smash. Three gargantuan brachios dashed out from the trees. The guard fired at them, but either he missed in his panic, or his bullets were ineffectual against the thick hides of these aged saurs. To his astonishment Poppo Miguel was running alongside the one in front, his legs beating the undergrowth wildly. 'Go, go, go!' he yelled, urging it on. The guard who'd been left behind turned heel and bolted down the hillside as fast as his legs could carry him to avoid being crushed.

Poppo Miguel held out his arms and the saurs went round him, so as to avoid trampling Javier, who lay terrified on the ground trying to shield his head. Behind the three saurs the other two guards were learning very quickly that this was absolutely the wrong place to be if you wanted to avoid being whacked senseless by three powerful brachio tails.

◆ ◆ ◆

'What on earth?' Theodore cried as the ground above them began to shake with the impressive weight of the three saurs as they bounded towards the hole.

Theodore and Bea craned their necks to try to see what was going on. It seemed to Bea as if the roof was about to cave in and she let out a shriek. Budge whipped his head about and stomped his feet. Then the thundering stopped, and when the dust cleared Poppo Miguel's head appeared, alongside those of three brachios.

Breathing heavily, the old man called down, 'It's time for us to leave!'

Poppo Miguel had brought the brachios to a skidding halt at the edge of the hole. Budge recoiled momentarily,

as if shocked to meet his own kind up close and so unexpectedly, and began honking. Carter tried to calm him down, patting his flank and saying, 'Hush! Hush!'

Some vine ropes dropped down, and they tried their best to attach the end of the ropes to Budge, but when they attempted to move him it was apparent that he was too big to be lifted out. The three fully grown brachios had the strength to do it, but the vines and rope did not. The vines split apart and the rope unravelled and broke under the punk's weight. Their failed effort brought another deluge of rocks and earth upon them, but this gave Theodore an idea.

'Enlarge the hole!' he called up.

Poppo Miguel instructed the brachios to carefully stomp on an area adjacent to the hole with their hind legs, and, sure enough, the edges started to give way. Theodore and Bea took shelter in an alcove, and when the stomping stopped they emerged to see more daylight streaming in from above. What's more, the pile of debris had now grown large enough to enable Budge to get a better foothold and start to climb out himself. The final part was a greater challenge, but Poppo Miguel instructed the wild brachios to lower their huge heads and help push the punk up further so that he eventually flopped out of the hole and slumped from the exhaustion.

'You appear to be fine,' Poppo Miguel said, once they had clambered up.

'What's been going on up here?' Theodore demanded. 'Where are the guards?'

'Poppo!' Bea exclaimed. 'How did you manage that? And how is Javier?'

'I have some tricks up my sleeve,' Poppo Miguel said, turning towards her. 'It's good to see you, Beatrice,' he said. 'My grandson told me you were pretty, and he was right.'

'How long have you been able to see?' she uttered in disbelief.

'A little while now,' he replied as they tended to Javier, 'thanks to young Carter here.'

'Who, me?' Carter said.

'You gave me a new eye, didn't you?' Poppo Miguel replied. 'What else was it for?'

'But I didn't think – I mean, I didn't know it could actually help you see,' Carter spluttered. 'After all, it's made of stone.'

'Yes, but a very special stone, isn't it?' Poppo Miguel said. 'A keystone has power only if it is given freely. You gave it to me for my sight, so now I am able to see with its help,' he said as if this was common sense.

'Where did these brachios come from?' Carter asked.

'Please meet the three *abuelas*,' Poppo Miguel said. 'These old grandmothers are old friends of mine.'

'Mama?' Javier called out. 'Mama!'

'He has a fever,' Bea said, her voice loaded with worry. 'He's getting worse!'

'We have to find Lucia,' Theodore said. 'It sounded like the General was taking her back to the avocado plantation, which is odd, since that's exactly where the Rebel area is marked on our map. I don't suppose –'

'Hurry,' Bea urged. 'We have to get back to town to find a doctor.'

'And get Buster back!' Carter exclaimed.

Poppo Miguel stopped her. 'Not so fast.'

'But Javier is hurting badly,' Bea protested, 'and he's already had to wait too long.'

'And the General will be back to raid this place,' Theodore reminded them. 'It's not safe to remain a moment longer.'

'Everything we need to heal him is close by,' Poppo Miguel said calmly. 'And it's better than a doctor could ever be. Only then can we look for Lucia.' He paused. 'She's a strong woman,' he said, as if convincing himself. 'But first, it is best if I do this.'

Poppo Miguel took from his pocket a small twig with a few leaves. 'I went in search of this before summoning the three *abuelas* here,' he explained. 'Watch,' he told Carter, who was soothing Budge by laying his cheek against his neck 'and learn.'

He then urged Budge to open his mouth, and making soft sounds, jabbed the twig at the back of his throat, making him momentarily gag.

'Hey!' Bea said, but Poppo Miguel withdrew his hand, and she could see that the end of the tree cutting was dripping with saliva. Poppo Miguel then walked over to the edge of the hole, all eyes curious as to what he was about to do.

'This will keep the city lost for ever,' he said, and carefully planted the cutting into the loose earth.

Right before their eyes the cutting appeared to take root, as if what they were watching was a speeded-up film. It reminded Bea of the way scenes shot past on the projector when the reel was coming to an end, the way they had when Monty Lomax had shown them films in Kenya. It was remarkable; they watched astonished as new leaves began to appear.

Bea's eyes grew wide, and she rubbed them as if waking from a dream. But it was real.

'This is now a very special tree,' Poppo Miguel explained. 'Only a true Saurman will be able to find it. To anyone else, it will be as if this place does not exist. We will let it lie in peace.'

'But, Poppo,' said Bea urgently, 'what about Javier?'

'Now it is his turn to be healed,' agreed Poppo Miguel, turning away from the sapling. 'Follow me.'

21

The Nest

~ powerful medicine ~

The charging brachios had made a pathway of broken branches that made it easy for Javier to be carried on the stretcher through the dense jungle.

Carter felt wretched without Buster by his side. 'We have to get him back,' he said firmly. 'I'm not leaving without Buster.'

'I know,' Theodore replied. 'Don't worry, Carter – we'll do our best to find him – and Lucia – just as soon as Javier is out of danger, you have my word.'

Carter nodded. He was too upset to speak. He was terribly troubled by having to trust that the advice of others was the best course of action, and yet, just as he had experienced with the Ronax in Kenya, having faith in future plans was something people sometimes had to have.

It wasn't long before they came to a large clearing in the jungle that was bathed in late-afternoon sunlight. It was the strangest sight Bea, Carter and Theodore had seen since arriving in this lush and colourful country. There were signs that many brachios had passed through this space, as the trees were all well cropped back – but a single ancient tree remained in the centre of the clearing. It soared into the sky, its trunk as thick as a brachiosaur's body and its branches as thick as their hind legs.

Bea remarked that even the bark of the tree looked like the gnarled old skin of the *abuelas*, who now stood

beside it. 'This tree has obviously never been trimmed by a brachio,' she noted.

Around the tree were lush meadows of flowers and ferns, unusual for the middle of the jungle. Immediately surrounding the tree the greenery gave way to a series of grooves hollowed out of the ground, which were lined with moss and bracken and filled with the broken shells of countless brachiosaur eggs.

'It looks exactly like the temple on my map!' Bea exclaimed to Poppo Miguel with pleasure.

'Told you so,' he said, smiling. 'It's good to be able to see it again.' He waved his hand towards where Bea and Carter were staring and offered up an explanation. 'The green pasture surrounding this tree is probably the most

fertile earth in all of Mexico,' he said. 'The brachios trim back the jungle to let the light bathe it, eating the big plants to provide the smaller, juicier plants space to thrive. This brings different creatures to this place and they all are protected by the sacred tree.'

A butterfly fluttered past Carter and landed on Bea's nose to her delight. Then it moved on to join the thousand others that filled the warm air.

They made their way to the shade of the tree and turned their attention towards Javier, who had fallen into a feverish sleep.

'A ceremony Javier underwent shortly after birth in this place bonds the human with the saurs,' Poppo Miguel explained. 'It protects them from harm and extends their life. My father brought me here when I was born, and his father before that. Now it is time to save him by using that same protection.'

'But how?' Bea asked, finding a spot to sit and do some sketching of the tranquil location. She wanted to record what she could remember of the underground chamber while it was fresh in her mind. This place, too, provided a wonderful opportunity to make a lasting impression in her book.

Before she received an answer, the ground trembled as the *abuelas* let out a series of honks that reverberated all around them.

'The *abuelas* are calling the hatchlings,' Poppo

Miguel explained.

Bea looked up at the saurs' deeply wrinkled skin as they gently ambled around the clearing, straightening their trunk-like necks as they let out more honks. They looked majestic.

'Why do you call them *abuelas?*' Carter asked.

'That's what they are,' Poppo Miguel replied. 'Elderly females tend to the eggs and then the hatchlings who emerge from them. The parents leave their eggs to be tended by them. If they stayed they would strip the jungle around here of everything, and then there would be nothing for the hatchlings to eat. When these juveniles start to grow their spiky head crests, they must be reunited with the adults before they become punks, as they are too unruly for the *abuelas* to cope with.'

'Like looking after teenagers,' Theodore commentated under his breath.

Bea and Carter noticed smaller brachios picking up the courage to venture out from their hiding places in the jungle. One by one, the bravest walked into the clearing, but once they spotted humans in the vicinity they paused, and issued forth a series of loud warning honks to the others.

'Looks like these wild brachios have never seen humans before, unlike Budge who probably thinks he is one,' Theodore said, as he gazed up at the fine creatures.

Out from the jungle came several more juvenile

punks who stood skittishly waiting near the trees. They approached cautiously, with the largest of them already sporting a full crest of head spikes, turning its head to sniff them all out individually. Everyone stood rooted to the spot, humbled by the sheer number and size of these saurs, but not afraid. Budge became excited and playful but one of the *abuelas* who was keeping an eye on his unruly antics gently calmed him with a few slaps of her tail.

'Help me carry the boy,' Poppo Miguel said to Theodore, and they lifted him over to an indentation that appeared longer than the rest. 'Bea – fetch some fresh bracken,' he instructed, and when she had returned they laid Javier in a nest of his own and retreated to watch what would happen.

The punks and *abuelas* all moved in and engulfed Javier for some time. The only sounds which could be heard were gentle slurps as the saurs licked him all over.

'This only works if you underwent the ritual as a child,' Poppo Miguel explained. 'Otherwise all this means nothing, has no effect. Something special in the saurs' saliva bonds with the infant and makes them a Saurman for life.'

'Just like me!' Carter exclaimed. 'The clan of shadow raptors who took me kept me in their nest for a long time. It was the only home I knew until I was old enough to crawl.'

'No wonder your gifts are so natural and strong,' said Poppo Miguel, understanding at last.

'It's where I took you after you'd been shot,' Carter told Theodore. 'I figured that if it always healed me, it would heal you, too.'

'And it did,' Theodore said. He rotated his arm round and looked to it. 'I couldn't believe how fast it healed. I have a faint memory of waking up while the shadow raptors were licking me, although at the time I thought they were eating me!'

'Remember you said the soles of your feet were licked clean after they froze on the ship, too,' Bea reminded him.

'I knew you were a Saurman when I first met you,' Poppo Miguel added, 'though I feel that you have denied this for a long time. Do you still doubt yourself?'

'People keep telling me I am – and I feel the power of my keystone and have connected with some saurs – but how can I be a Saurman?' Theodore responded. 'I was born in the East End of London, not in a jungle near a sacred tree. No one passed down any wisdom to me; I was given my keystone by Sidney Brownlee, the children's grandfather. He was wise and showed me how to be a man, but not a Saurman.'

'None of that matters,' Poppo Miguel said kindly. 'To be a true Saurman – someone who can benefit from the life-giving healing abilities – you need to be bonded with saurs from birth.'

'My father was in the business of cutting saurs up, not conducting ceremonies with them,' Theodore scoffed. 'He was a saurmonger, not a healer or a wise man.'

Poppo Miguel shook his head. 'Let me explain what it is I know,' he said, and took a deep breath.

'Only pure breed or wild saurs possess the crucial germs in their glands which are passed on to their young. They do this by licking them clean and feeding them regurgitated food. It is the same for many saurs, birds and reptiles. These are some of the oldest species alive on this earth; they have evolved many ways to outlive all the other species who come and go.'

'What about farmed saurs, why don't they have the special germs in their glands?' asked Bea, who was paying close attention.

'Most farmed animals don't have the chance to bond this way with their parents. When you take the eggs from a saur's nest and incubate them you are breaking the chain that connects them to their parents, who don't get to lick them clean or feed them.'

Theodore nodded. 'Farmed animals certainly have shorter and less fulfilling lives.'

'If what you say is true –' Poppo Miguel pointed at Theodore – 'and you have been healed in this way, then you must have been licked by saurs when you were a baby.'

Theodore began to shake his head no, but stopped. 'Wait a minute,' he began. 'Now that I think about it . . .'

He sank to his knees, lost in thought.

It was a while before Theodore spoke, and when he did his voice was choked with emotion. 'My father never let me forget it . . .' he began haltingly. 'My mother, she had a hard time delivering me, they said. By the time I was born she was exhausted and didn't think she could go on. But she wasn't done yet; there was a complication and they had to cut her open. She died before she ever set eyes on me.' Theodore looked away. 'My oldest brothers taunted me, saying that I should have died. That if I had, their mother would still be alive instead of me. I think there was another baby that became stuck, and neither of them made it.'

Bea placed a loving hand on her godfather's back.

'My father resented my existence. My brothers slept upstairs above the butcher shop, but my place was below, near the old ice cupboard. I shared a bed with Champion, and before that Lady, my pet phalox, But there were times when –' he paused, trying to find the right words – 'the saurs treated me more like their own than my family did. I suppose they might have licked me as a very young child.'

'So we are not so different after all,' Poppo Miguel said simply.

22

It's What's Inside

~ empty shells ~

The next day, Javier slept in his nest while his ankle healed. Bea kept watch over him attentively and took the opportunity to leaf back through her mother's sketchbook and process all that she had learnt in the last few days.

Theodore sat next to her. Bea was growing up, becoming more like her mother every day. Grace had been such a kind soul. 'Show me what you've been sketching,' he said.

Bea eagerly turned round her sketchbook. It wasn't often that Theodore showed an interest; he was usually too busy exploring for himself. She started with what she could recall of the titanosaur's jewelled skull, which was embellished with a riot of colours to represent the gems.

'You're as talented as your dear mother,' Theodore said admiringly.

'I was just showing her drawings to Javier the other day,' Bea replied wistfully. 'I wish she could have seen mine.'

'I sincerely regret having moved that skull,' said Theodore. 'Carter was right; I should have listened to him. Now look whose hands it's in. That's the last thing I wanted. Not only that, but they have Lucia and Buster. I don't know how we're going to be able to get them back.' He slumped, holding his head in his hands. 'I've messed up, big time,' he moaned, anguish in his voice.

Bea put her arm round his shoulders. 'It's going to be okay,' she said. 'We all mess up from time to time.'

◆ ◆ ◆

Even though Poppo Miguel had answered almost all of the questions Bea had about the Saurmen, his explanations had opened the door to yet more, so she moved closer to the curious old man who was resting under the sacred temple tree.

'Forgive me for asking this again, Poppo,' said Bea, 'but you, Javier, Carter and Theodore are Saurmen because you've all been licked by saurs as infants, correct?'

'Yes,' Poppo Miguel replied, 'but we're not all the same. Saurmen around the world are all different because they have different temple trees, live amongst different saurs, and probably have slightly different ceremonies. Javier and I had brachiosaurs lick us; Carter had shadow raptors – and Theodore tells me he had a phalox!'

'I wasn't licked by a saur at birth,' Bea said quietly, 'but I do have a keystone. Theodore has one, and now you have one that Carter gave you, replacing the one your family lost, which has allowed you to see again.' She became more upbeat.

'What is your question, young girl?' Poppo Miguel asked.

'Does my keystone also make me a Saurman?' she asked. 'Or a Saurwoman? I've felt a connection with it, just like Theodore describes.'

'The keystones are one thing and having the ability to heal is another,' the old man ventured. 'They are two separate things. But perhaps neither ability alone makes a Saurman.' He tapped his chest with his thin fingers. 'Perhaps it's what's inside here.' He winked at her.

Bea understood, but Poppo Miguel could see she wanted a firmer answer.

'People have always asked the same questions, and no one has been able to answer them completely,' Poppo Miguel added. 'A very long time ago, I knew of some bad people who could command saurs to do their bidding. They had keystones and learnt how to use them, but they were not Saurmen – far from it. I have also known people who have no keystones and who possess no life-extending abilities, yet they can connect with animals and saurs in the same way.'

Bea clicked her fingers as something popped into her head. 'I know a man called Wolf,' she said, her eyes wide. 'He has a bear he talks to and he loves Great Zinos. He's dedicated his life to looking after them.'

'I thought the Great Zino was extinct?' Poppo Miguel remarked.

'Not any more, thanks to Wolf.'

Poppo Miguel looked impressed. 'I know a kind man who befriends all stray dogs and feeds them. There is also a man in the next village who has a special way with horses.' He leant in close and said softly, 'Whispers to them, he does.'

Bea giggled back at him. 'That reminds me of Carter,' she said. 'But he doesn't have a keystone of his own – he keeps giving his away.'

'Your brother has a generous heart,' Poppo Miguel said.

'So it's about love, compassion and friendship,' Bea stated boldly, more sure of herself.

Poppo Miguel nodded. 'I believe so. ' He pointed to her

keystone. 'And having one of those magnifies what is already inside you. The bigger the heart, the more powerful it is.'

Bea felt her keystone glow a little as the old man said the words and her heart trembled with delight. She looked over at Theodore who was with Carter amongst the juvenile brachios. 'And it certainly helps if you can heal faster when you keep getting into scrapes or being shot at by thugs.'

'Absolutely,' Poppo Miguel agreed. 'But I think there is no magic in it. I know very little about science but I'm sure that one day someone will work out how you can extract the right fluids from saurs' saliva to harness that ability.'

Bea was happy that she had managed to have this time with Poppo Miguel and get all the facts straight in her head. 'How old are you, Poppo?' she asked.

Poppo Miguel laughed. 'I can't remember, to be honest.' He looked up at the three *abuelas*. 'But I remember when they were punks!'

✦ ✦ ✦

Later, as they were resting after eating and waiting for Javier to heal, Carter made an observation. 'If this is a nest,' he said, 'then why are there no new shells? The ones around here are all old.'

'You're right,' Poppo Miguel agreed. 'That's because they are last year's crop,' he explained. 'The juveniles which came to lick Javier's wounds were also older than I expected them to be, and still living with the *abuelas*, rather than the pack they should have joined. I'm a Brachio Saurman,' he said solemnly. 'My duty is to protect these saurs, and I have been away for too long. Where are the other packs of adults that would normally have returned here to lay new eggs and lead away the mature hatchlings? This is something I am duty-bound to find out, and to help if I can.'

'Perhaps the Rebels are to blame,' Bea said, 'by encroaching on their territory.'

'You may be right,' Poppo Miguel said. 'Those cleared circles we saw from the ridge – I have a hunch that is where we should start looking. They looked like trouble to me.'

◆ ◆ ◆

Javier's eyes flicked open. 'Where am I?' he asked Bea, who knelt over him. His voice was still slurred from the deeply sedated state he'd been in. 'Where's Mama?'

'She's not here,' Bea replied hesitantly. 'I'm sure Lucia's okay, though.'

'What do you mean?' Javier said, trying to get up. 'Where is she? Where am I?'

'Not so fast!' Bea cautioned him. 'You've been unconscious for quite a while. 'We're at the temple tree,' she told him. 'The brachiosaur nest.'

Javier looked puzzled, and tried to focus his eyes on his strange surroundings.

'Poppo brought you here after you broke your ankle,' Bea explained.

Javier reached down to feel his ankle, as if he'd been unaware of his injury. 'Right,' he said shakily. 'I remember now – we'd fallen into a sinkhole – we were pulled out – and men came . . .' Here he paused. 'My mother! They took her! Bea, where is she?' He scrambled to get up once again.

Theodore had noticed what was going on and come over. 'How's the patient?' he asked.

'Never mind about me – what about Mama?' Javier cried. 'We have to find her!'

'That's just what we're going to do,' Theodore replied, 'as soon as you're fit to walk. Let's feel that ankle of yours.'

It was astonishing; Javier's ankle was far less swollen, and the cuts it had sustained were nearly healed over. Bea prodded gently to feel for any sore spots, and to Javier's amazement there were none. His ankle even seemed strong enough to take a little weight, so he was helped up, and with Theodore and Bea for support managed to hobble over to their camp amongst the outer ring of brachio nests.

'Now that Javier's on the mend, can we go get Buster?' Carter asked.

'First Lucia, then Buster,' Theodore replied. 'Then the jewelled skull – in that order.'

'What say you, Saurmen?' Poppo Miguel declared. 'Do you want to find out what's going on around here?'

As everyone nodded their assent, Bea pointed to the red-lined area marking the Rebel encampment on the map. 'Let's go,' she said.

23

Freeing the Brachios

~ releasing prisoners ~

Making their way down towards the clearings took some time. Without Buster to ride on, Carter helped Theodore and Bea lead the way. Javier continued to rest, riding with Poppo Miguel on Budge. While they rode, to take their minds off Lucia and what might be happening to her, Poppo Miguel filled the newcomers in on what the Gemini Festival was all about – after all, he had been on far more occasions than anyone else. The festival marked the prominence of the twins in the sky, the constellation known as Gemini. This was an especially auspicious time when harmony, especially between opposites, was felt to be most prominent amongst all living things. It had been believed that at one time the sun and stars had disappeared from the sky, and for days and days there was no darkness or daylight, just a dullness where nothing could grow and everything deteriorated. To bring the day and night back the king had made a great sacrifice for his people. This was a celebration of not just the very same ancient king who had reigned over the lost city that they had fallen into days earlier, but also of the twins, whom everyone now believes live to this day above them in the constellation of Gemini; Castor and Pollux, the two brightest stars. In the words of their good friend Ranjit, the impossible was possible. Not only had they been the only people to wander through the long-forgotten city, but they had actually met the actual twins at their resting place in North America, where they had been spirited away by the Saurmen.

'I'm sorry that I didn't pay attention to your tales of the Brachio Saurmen,' Javier said regretfully. 'It all seemed so far-fetched; now I have seen with my own eyes how real this power is, and what it can do.'

'I wish your father was still with us to see what a fine young man you've grown up to be,' said Poppo Miguel proudly.

'If Papa can't be here to teach me, can you, Poppo?' Javier asked. 'After all, one day, I might have a son of my own to pass this knowledge on to.'

'You're a natural at riding Budge,' Poppo Miguel noted, patting the saur's flank. 'But of course you'll need to have your own brachio if you are to be a Brachio Saurman.'

♦ ♦ ♦

By the early evening of the first day Javier's ankle was greatly improved and he was able to limp along using Poppo Miguel's walking stick and let the others take turns and rest on the brachio. They all wanted to keep going through

the night as every moment brought them closer to finding Lucia and Buster.

They approached the first circular clearing at dawn, just as the sun began to throw its golden light across the treetops. So far they had avoided paths, preferring to bend their way through the jungle in silence. Theodore and Carter led the way and found new routes with enough space to weave between trees, through thick undergrowth and to ford streams. They passed the warning notice that indicated where the red areas had been marked on Lambert's map. Their first glance into the circular space confirmed their fears: a fat brachio lay near the perimeter attached by a length of long chain. Theodore and Carter crept out to try to unpin it, but the thick steel chain was padlocked. Theodore tried to use the point of his knife in the lock but it was obvious that would not work.

'If only we had a –' Theodore was cut short as Carter opened up his satchel, removed the tobacco tin that contained the sum of his worldly possessions, and pulled out an old paperclip. 'I was going to say a key,' said Theodore, 'but that might work.'

'I found this in Aru,' Carter said. 'I never knew what it was for until I saw Monty Lomax use one in a film.'

'It's called a paperclip,' Theodore remarked. 'You usually use it to clip loose papers together.'

'Don't be silly,' Carter said, scrunching up his face. 'They're used to pick open locks.'

Thankfully it worked. Once the padlock was opened, the chain fell away, leaving a deep wound round the ankle caused by the mighty saur pulling on the chain. Carter checked the wound all over for infection. 'It will need licking clean for it to heal,' he noted as the brachio stood and craned its long neck down to inspect it and the strange boy who had freed it. Carter gently ran his hands round its muzzle. 'Go,' he whispered.

The brachio swung round, glanced at the punk at the edge of the trees, and majestically manoeuvred off out of the clearing that had been its prison for the last few weeks. They all watched in silence as the brachio slowly and silently disappeared into the dense undergrowth back to freedom. A wave of great relief washed over them and, energised, they pressed on to the next clearing, and the next, releasing each miserable creature in turn with Carter's paperclip key. Bea told Javier and Poppo Miguel all about the skeleton key she had made, which was carved from an old bone by copying an imprint made of the original key in wax.

As the sun rose they noticed amargas stirring in the next clearing and beginning to graze on the tender weeds and shoots that had popped up in the night.

'It's without doubt an illegal farming operation,' said Theodore, 'and on a grand scale.'

'Mama said her job at the plantation was to make sure the amargas cleared away the new shoots while the loggers removed the timber,' Javier remembered. 'Only then could the avocado trees be planted.'

'These saurs should be free to roam,' said Poppo Miguel, 'not be penned in to work for man. This is what happened to the ancient people whose city we found. Eventually this will all end badly, like it did for them.'

The amargas were only tethered by rope as they did not require heavy chains to restrain them. Theodore gave Bea his knife and Carter used his two sharpened raptor claws to slice them and set the saurs free. It was an immensely satisfying sight when the captive saurs realised they could roam free and leave the clearings. One by one they leapt and twisted into the air, shaking out the two rows of long spines that ran down their backs.

'They're doing binkies!' Bea exclaimed.

Javier and Carter looked at her quizzically.

'Rabbits do them when they're happy,' she explained. 'They randomly leap about and twist, just like that.' She pointed at another armarga who twirled into the air with delight.

'They're jumping for joy!' said Javier.

'She's right,' said Poppo Miguel, 'but I have only heard of this happening; I've never witnessed this before.' He placed a hand on Carter's shoulder. 'Thank you for giving me the opportunity to see again,' he said.

The next circle they came to gave them an answer as to why the clearings were there. In this there was fresh grass growing on the cleared land, and grazing happily upon it were a small herd of very young tritop calves. Their new white skin was thin and supple and had a maroon tint to it from the dark flesh beneath.

Bea crept up close to pat one. 'You're a little cutie,' she said, as it licked the salty sweat from her hand. Carter sat next to her and let one come over to him. He gently ran his hands over its short frill and stubby nose.

'Those blunt stubs will become long horns one day,' Bea remarked.

'But it won't live to be a fully grown adult,' Theodore corrected her. 'Just fat enough to fetch a good price at the market,' he said solemnly. 'It won't ever know its mother or run freely.' When Theodore crept closer to inspect them he noticed that they were Californian Longhorn Tritops of the kind Cash and the ranchers had raised. 'Strange,' he said. 'Rubeosaurs with the long nose horn are usually found in this region. These have obviously been imported.'

'Why do that?' asked Javier.

'Californian Longhorn Tritops are bigger and the meat sells for more. I have a feeling we won't be finding any avocado trees,' Theodore concluded. 'This is a tritop farm.'

By now the sun was fully up and voices could be heard coming from the main clearing. Before they could see anything, they could smell and hear a generator

chugging out fumes and running electricity to a group of low buildings. There was a large wooden water tower and surrounding this a series of tents with farm hands milling about around getting ready for a normal day's work.

'Look!' Carter exclaimed in a hushed voice. 'Buster!' He was roped up in a small paddock with another saur, a Mountain Tyrant.

Carter whipped the binoculars from his satchel to get a better look. Beyond the tyrants was a second pen, which contained pale and dark green striped Irritators.

Theodore pointed out to Bea the long wooden building. 'Something important is in there,' he reasoned – 'it's being powered by the generator.'

Bea studied the glassless windows, which were covered with wire nets to keep insects out. She pointed to a set at the end. 'Those windows have metal bars – could that be where Lucia is being kept prisoner?'

Suddenly the door swung open and out stepped General Vulpez, who lit a cigar and marched over towards a group of men all dressed in drab mismatched camouflage uniforms.

'Look, more Rebels,' whispered Bea.

Making sure they remained hidden, everyone quietly watched as some of the Rebels put the finishing touches to two old army trucks that had been crudely decorated with white paint to resemble the skeletons of full-size tritops.

'I bet they're planning to upset the Gemini Festival,' said Javier. 'Everyone in the parade has to be in pairs, and that's a pair of army-truck tritops!'

'But I'm confused,' said Bea. 'If that rotten General is with the army, why is he helping the Rebels?'

'It's probably all part of a double-cross,' said Theodore, who was now looking through Carter's binoculars. 'Some of them are in army uniforms. They're probably just pretending to be Rebels to keep people away from this place.'

The labourers, meanwhile, had picked up their tools and started wandering away from the tents and off to work.

'We get one shot at this and we have to be quick,' said Bea. 'The farmers will soon find all the brachios and amargas have been set free.' Everyone nodded. 'So what's the plan, Theo?' she asked.

Theodore looked surprised. 'I didn't make one,' he replied sheepishly. 'What about you – any ideas?'

Bea shook her head. Javier shrugged. Everyone turned to Carter, who looked away quickly at Budge.

'I have an idea,' said Poppo Miguel.

24

What's All the Racket?

~ a new prisoner ~

Suddenly two bursts from a whistle shot out across the clearing. 'Stray brachio, coming this way!' a voice called out.

The General swung round and saw a punk brachio bounding over towards the water tower.

'Ropes, bring plenty of ropes!' he ordered. 'We have a new recruit!'

His guards dashed to pick up coils of rope and prepared to capture the saur thundering towards them.

'Strange – it has a harness!' muttered one guard as he threw the first lasso, missing his head. From another angle two more lassos flew through the air but again Budge dodged them. The fourth was on target, but as it tightened midway down its neck the man on the other end was jerked forward and let go. More of the General's guards readied themselves and soon ropes were being tossed all over the place in the vain hope that some would hit their mark.

Quickly becoming distressed, the punk swung round and took out three guards and part of the wooden support

holding up the water tower with its tail.

A loud *CRACK!* sounded as the whole structure jolted forward.

Momentarily distracted, Budge stood over a lasso that had fallen to the ground. It was quickly pulled tight. Three men ran the other end round the bumper of a truck and the metal creaked as it took the strain.

Another lasso hit its target and then another landed over its head. Men were being pulled up into the air as Budge swung his head round, so a guard tied the end of his rope to the base of the water tower. As soon as he tightened the knot, the General shouted at him, 'Untie that, you stupid –' But he was cut short. The enraged Budge yanked hard, and there came another loud *CRACK* of twisting wood.

The tower swayed, spilling some of its contents in a waterfall, drenching the man beneath.

'Cut that rope!' the General cried, but it was too late – the tower rocked backwards and for a moment held its balance, before the vast weight of water sloshing about

forced it just past the tipping point.

As the commotion raged outside Theodore peered through the window of the door leading into the long wooden hut and saw the coast was clear to head inside. He gently opened the door and waved to Bea and Javier to follow him.

Inside, row upon row of tritop eggs lay in their man-made nests under the warmth of overhead lights that flickered from time to time when the generator spluttered.

'It's a hatchery!' Bea whispered.

Close to the entrance was a large empty wooden crate that had straw inside and a newly hatched tritop calf lay dozing under the warm lamp. It was clearly the same

type as the ones they'd found in the clearing. Bea looked closer and waved to get Theodore's attention. 'Theo! These crates say the Sauria Firearms Corporation – isn't that Lambert's company?'

'Is your friend the one who brought over all these eggs?' Javier asked in dismay.

'Impossible,' Theodore cut in as he came over. 'These could be old crates taken from somewhere else. I expect many armies buy their guns from him. He's a very successful businessman.'

'Yes, I doubt he knows the details of every deal his companies make,' Bea agreed. 'We should warn Lambert his crates are being used this way, though,' she said seriously. 'He'd be so upset to think his company was associated with illegal farming.'

I wonder if he knows that rat General Vulpez is part of it? pondered Theodore, as he noticed a door at the other end of the building bolted with a large lock. 'That must be the room with bars over the window,' he said. 'Hang back and stay hidden until I give you the all-clear.' With that he made his way carefully towards the locked door.

Off the long room with the rows of incubating eggs were more doorways. Some of the doors were open and Theodore could see that some were stocked with provisions and all manner of scientific equipment and jars on shelves. He crept up to the door and slid the bolt open as quietly as he could and peered inside. It was unlit, but Theodore could make out some old sacks and a figure curled up on them.

'Lucia, thank goodness you're safe!'

Upon hearing Theodore's voice Lucia scrambled to stand up, but could not raise her hands as they were chained to the steel bars in the window set into the wooden wall.

'Unlock me!' she whispered urgently.

'Who has the key?' Theodore asked, kicking himself for giving Carter his paperclip back.

'The General,' Lucia replied. 'Can't you just shoot the lock?' she asked, pointing to the pistol by his side.

Theodore shrugged. 'It's not loaded.'

'You carry an empty gun?'

'If we get out of here, I'll explain,' said Theodore. 'Wait here,' he added as he ran back out into the hatchery.

'I have no other choice!' muttered Lucia frantically.

'Your mother is safe, but chained up,' Theodore said as he rejoined Bea and Javier. 'We have no way of picking the lock, though.'

'What do we do?' Javier asked anxiously.

'We can try to get Buster to smash the wall down and break her out,' Theodore suggested.

'Would that work?'

'Buster's always smashing things up,' Theodore replied, 'only this time it won't be by mistake. Quick – he should be still there in the paddock.'

Bea darted outside. Theodore peered out of the window and saw that Budge was now pulling several of the guards through a huge puddle of mud where the water tower once stood.

'Buster's not the only saur who's good at smashing things,' Theodore muttered.

* * *

'What's all the racket?' came a voice from one of the rooms off the hatchery and out stepped a man with round dark spectacles.

'*Que?*' quick-thinking Theodore said in as good a Mexican accent as he could muster.

'Never mind, another one is about to hatch.' He waved Theodore over. 'Come and get it.'

'*Si, señor.*' Theodore hobbled over, trying not to make eye contact with the man who was pointing to an egg with a crack. It wobbled a little and another crack appeared. The man took two elbow-length rubber gloves from his belt and slipped his hands inside.

'Gloves?' he asked as Theodore nervously looked up. 'Get your gloves – it's pure! The last thing I want is your dirty hands on it.' He pointed back to the door where several pairs of gloves were hanging on hooks.

Theodore had no choice but to continue playing along. He was just taking some gloves when the door swung open and standing in front of Theodore was Christian Hayter.

* * *

'What do you mean?' barked General Vulpez.

'It's gone, I tell you,' said one of the guards, who'd just returned from the lost city, where he'd been sent with a crew of excavators to expand the sinkhole. 'There's nothing there – no hole, no people, no brachio, no lost city. There are only flattened places where people had been.'

The General spat his cigar out at the man. 'Impossible – did you follow your tracks back?'

'*Si*, General,' the man said, 'but they led us around in circles.'

'Are you all blind? I saw the place with my own eyes – there was a huge hole in the ground with a brachio in it,' the General hissed. 'How could that *disappear?*'

'I promise you, General – we spread out and looked around several times. You are welcome to look for yourself. It's gone.'

As the General was considering what punishment to inflict on his incompetent guards his attention was suddenly caught by the punk brachio causing mayhem outside. 'It has a saddle, neck reins and a head mount with tassels!' he declared. 'It's the punk from the hole!'

General Vulpez swung round towards the hatchery, just as a grinning Hayter emerged, dragging Theodore Logan behind him and brandishing his vicious bullhook.

'Guards, restrain that brachio,' the General barked. 'You!' He jabbed the guard in front of him. 'Help Señor Hayter with our new prisoner.'

The General lit another cigar then turned on his heels and walked off towards the paddock, waving two men to follow him.

◆ ◆ ◆

Ash and Bishop laughed as yet more men joined in trying to lasso and restrain Budge. As he spun round, it looked like the people trying to restrain him were on a strange merry-go-round.

'Go on then,' said Ash. 'Show 'em how to do it.' He patted Bishop on the shoulder.

Bishop cracked his knuckles. 'Sure the boss won't mind?'

Ash shook his head. 'Go for it – get in the practice. I would.'

'I'll show the amateurs how to do it,' Bishop muttered as he withdrew a knuckleduster from his back pocket and strode over. The Irritators stirred a little when the light caught the keystone inlaid into it.

◆ ◆ ◆

'It's no good – we'll be spotted,' said Bea. 'One's gone, but the skinny chap's still there. We'll never get close enough to Buster to free him without being seen.'

'Where's Carter?' Javier asked.

'Nowhere!' Bea said, worried.

Javier peered round the other side of the stack of gasoline barrels to see if he could spot Bea's brother, but quickly retreated and tugged on her elbow. 'Get back, the General's coming!' he warned.

25

Christian Hayter

~ that horrid little man ~

'So today went well,' Christian Hayter purred, slurping his coffee. 'I got my Beast back – now I have two to choose from.'

'Buster's not the beast – you are!' Theodore spat.

'The saurboy renamed my tyrant, did he?' Hayter said, taking another swig. 'Buster and Buttercup; Buttercup and Buster. Nah – doesn't work for me. I like Buttercup and the Beast better.'

Theodore had a thousand questions. 'So you're working for General Vulpez now?'

Hayter just laughed.

'You've moved on from trading Raptor of Paradise feathers, I see.' Theodore raised his eyebrows. 'Found it tough poaching big game in Kenya, did you? Spot of bother helping dubious diamond miners?' He looked around. 'Correct me if I'm wrong here, but this is a tritop farm, and not remotely legal.'

'You missed something,' said Hayter, who looked out at the makeshift paddock, where the two tyrants were tied up and snapping at each other.

Theodore nodded. 'Of course,' he said, 'you must have been in California, too. How else would you have a Mountain Tyrant? I suppose you had something to do with all those saurs that kept getting killed near Cash Kingsley's ranch?'

Hayter nodded. 'Guilty as charged,' he admitted. 'I must say – the Kingsley ranch was delightful. The rancher's lovely wife even made me lemonade one afternoon.' He grinned as if relishing the memory.

Theodore shook with rage as Hayter smiled.

'You should turn round more often, Logan,' Hayter said. 'I've been right behind you all the way from Aru.'

'Then I have been one step ahead of you the whole time,' Theodore retorted.

Hayter just grinned and looked him up and down. 'Do you remember the first time we met?'

'Of course. You were fighting a defenceless shadow raptor in your depot on Aru,' said Theodore, 'and I regrettably helped you tie it up.'

'Now look who's all tied up!' Hayter pointed out. 'But you're wrong: we first met long before then, back in the East End of London.'

Theodore shook his head. 'We never met, but there was plenty of scum like you about.'

'It's funny,' Hayter continued, 'because after I met you on Aru it came to me: Logan's the saurmonger in

Plaistow.' He breathed in deeply through his nose. 'How could I forget that place? It was disgusting; it stunk real bad.' Hayter wafted his hand in front of his face.

Theodore was silent.

'Come on – you must remember,' Hayter teased.

'You should have smelt it on the inside,' Theodore said. 'I know – I lived there.'

'You had a pet phalox,' Hayter remarked.

'There were two – Lady and Champion,' Theodore replied.

'I remember just the one,' Hayter mused. 'It chased me into an alley, got me cornered and butted me badly.'

'That would have been Champion,' Theodore said grudgingly. 'He had the temper. You probably deserved it; what did you steal?'

'I pickpocketed some old man outside,' Hayter said dismissively. 'I can't remember the details.'

Theodore stared at the horrible little man in disbelief. 'So that was you!' he said through gritted teeth. 'The man you tried to pickpocket was Sidney Brownlee, late husband of the defenceless woman you later killed in Kenya.'

'Really?' Hayter said. 'I guess it's no surprise as our paths seem to keep crossing.'

'Perhaps we were destined to be enemies.' Theodore spoke coldly. 'I promise that you will pay for everything you have done.'

'And there I was in Kenya all tied up like you are now,'

Hayter taunted Theodore. 'At your mercy. And you didn't finish the job. But you're wrong about something. I didn't kill that old bat.'

'What do you mean?'

'I didn't kill Bunty Brownlee,' Hayter said, shaking his head. 'I should have killed her in Aru after I captured her, under that tree with the rainbow bark, when I had the chance.' Hayter pulled out his bullhook, rolled the polished metal head in his hand, and prodded Theodore's shoulder with the wooden handle. 'And my shot should have killed you, that's another regret I have.' He jabbed the handle viciously into Theodore's chest, but Theodore did not flinch.

'You don't have to lie to me, Hayter,' Theodore growled. 'You locked Bunty in the basement of the lodge when it was on fire. You killed her.'

'I've done and witnessed some bad things,' Hayter said, 'but that, I can assure you, I did not do.'

'Then who did?'

Hayter paused and looked Theodore directly in the eye. 'I wasn't the only person in the lodge when the fire broke out.'

'Liar!' Theodore shouted back at him. 'I promise you will pay for this!'

'Well, it's been pleasant catching up, but I'm done talking,' Hayter snapped, raising his bullhook and swinging it, just missing Theodore's face. 'You're not going to live past tomorrow, understand?'

Theodore stared Hayter down. His sworn enemy stood before him holding the bullhook menacingly, preparing to swing it a second time. He noticed the opal keystone set into the bullhook's metal head.

'Well, well, well – been using a little help, have you?' Theodore said contemptuously.

'Sure,' Hayter replied. 'And I'm not the only one. My men and the Doctor can all wield the power.'

'The Doctor. That would be the man in the dark glasses then,' Theodore remarked. 'I think you'll find that Carter took that man's power – his false eye – away from him the last time they met.'

Hayter scowled, annoyed that Logan knew more than he should.

'You're on *my* turf now,' Hayter said. 'Remember that.'

Theodore maintained a neutral expression. The Stegosorcerer's wise words echoed through his head: *this bad man, his path runs with yours.*

◆ ◆ ◆

Bea and Javier made it back to where Poppo Miguel was hiding.

'Poppo, it's all gone wrong!' Javier panted. 'We almost didn't make it out of there!'

'Some plan that was!' Bea exclaimed.

Poppo Miguel nodded. 'Then the plan was meant to fail – has no one been listening to me?'

Bea and Javier got their breaths back and looked at each other a little puzzled.

'What will be, will be – this is all part of our destiny,' the old man continued. 'Your failures will lead you to triumph.'

'We met a man in Kenya, the Stegosorcerer,' Bea commented, 'who said the same sort of crazy things. Except now it's not so crazy. Perhaps it's beginning to make sense.'

'Your brachio has been silenced,' Poppo Miguel noticed. 'What happened to him?'

They all listened quietly. There was no more commotion and they all gulped at the same time. Javier looked as distressed as Bea at the thought of Budge being captured, or injured, or worse. He'd come to care about the punk as much as Bea did.

'What do we do now, Poppo?' Javier asked his grandfather.

'I can't come up with ideas to save everyone every day,' he told them. 'You have to learn how to do it yourself – I'm old and one day I won't be here to help. It's time you became a Brachio Saurman, Javier. Fulfil your destiny.'

'But, Poppo,' Javier responded, 'I don't know how to do that. My father was taught by you how to be one. No one has taught me.'

'Nonsense,' Poppo Miguel replied. 'Everyone is learning all the time – have you not had your eyes open? Have you not been hearing?'

Javier tried to recall everything he'd been told, but shrugged. 'What was it you said?'

'Life is the teacher, not me,' Poppo Miguel reminded him. He turned to Bea. 'Please tell me you have been paying attention. What have you learnt, young Saurwoman?'

Bea loved being called a Saurwoman. It had a ring to it that dusted off the old ghosts of the past. She grabbed Javier by the arm. 'To fight their army, we summon an even greater saur army!'

'We can't make saurs fight our battles for us,' Javier said.

'Correct,' Poppo Miguel agreed.

'But –' Javier was gaining in confidence – 'we can outnumber them so that there's no battle,' he said, standing tall.

'Are you ready?' Bea asked. She leant in closer. 'Are you ready to fulfil your destiny?'

'I owe you an apology, Poppo,' Javier said, composing himself. 'I never took you seriously, and that was wrong. I can see now what your legacy means. Only you knew about the brachiosaur nest, and that it could heal me.'

Poppo Miguel smiled. 'Every Saurman benefits greatly

from a keystone.' He winked at Bea. 'I have a gift for you.' He pulled out of his shirt pocket the opal keystone eyeball Carter had given him and held it up, so that the light could set its dark surface ablaze in iridescent sparkles. Then he placed it into his grandson's hand and closed his fingers round it. 'Accept this gift. Carry it with you always, and use it to do good in the world and protect saurs whenever you get the opportunity. This is what being a Saurman means.'

'Poppo!' Javier exclaimed, a lump of emotion in this throat. 'Won't you become blind again?'

'I was happy blind,' Poppo Miguel said. 'My fingers led me, and other senses made up for my failed sight. Now being around all these keystones I can see a little, which is enough.' He tapped the opalised dinosaur bone keystone. 'This gift I must pass on to you, Javier, my grandson. I passed my original keystone to your father, but with him the chain was broken. My path will become complete if I pass this gift on to you. Now go – you have important things to do.'

26

The Hard Way or the Easy Way

~ *my big sister* ~

The General pushed Lucia to the ground. She winced as her knees scuffed the dirt beneath her. Hayter kicked Theodore in the back, knocking him down with a hard thud, but he scrambled to his knees beside Lucia. Things were desperate. He turned and gave her a weak blood-stained smile.

'Workers,' General Vulpez addressed the farmers who had been told to gather round the central clearing for an announcement. 'You are here to witness what happens when you disobey the rules of your employment.' He slowly scanned the clearing to make sure each of them caught his eye. 'And all I ask – all I have ever asked – is that you tell no one what goes on here.' He pointed to Lucia. 'Yet you, Señora Cantera, decided to tell this man –' he pointed to Theodore – 'and he decided to tell the authorities.'

All the farmers looked at each other uneasily.

'I know who you all are,' the General continued

menacingly. 'I know where you all live. I know where your children go to school. And I know when someone talks.' The General let the weight of his words hang in the air a long time.

The tension was palpable. The Doctor shuffled on the spot; Ash and Bishop tried not to look uneasy; and Hayter wiped the sweat from his brow.

'It doesn't have to be like this,' Theodore said loudly, breaking the silence.

Lucia looked at her friends and her fellow workers, and spoke up too. 'People, rise above this evil man,' she pleaded. 'This is not an avocado farm! That's a lie! Walk away from this place and tell everyone who he really is and what is going on here!'

The General crossed his arms and rocked back on his heels as if he was highly entertained. 'Carry on,' he drawled, 'you're just digging a deeper grave for yourself.'

Lucia was filled with rage. 'This man pretends to be an army general protecting the people,' she cried. 'He pretends to be the leader of the Rebels fighting for the people, yet he is neither. He is just a man taking from you and your country. Alone we are weak, but together we are strong. Rise up so all our voices can be heard together!'

The farmers remained huddled together.

The General started a slow clap, mocking her.

Theodore turned to Lucia. 'That was some speech,' he said in admiration.

The General's clapping came to an end, but as he stepped forward, someone in the assembled group continued to clap.

The General spun round to see who it was. 'You!' he barked, pointing to the elderly man with the kind face. 'Join your friends here,' he commanded.

But the man had started something, and his friend next to him started to clap as well.

'Both of you! Now!' the General demanded. Neither man moved. But more and more of the farmers joined in, clearly moved by Lucia's speech. Suddenly they were all clapping.

'*Basta!*' the General shouted. 'Enough! Señor Hayter, set your tyrant on these two.' He pointed at Theodore and Lucia. The clapping immediately died down. 'Then I will decide if any others will be its dessert.'

A single pair of hands could be heard still slowly clapping in the clearing. The person brave enough to defy the General's threat stepped forward. It was Carter. He had quietly blended in with the farmers rather than run away.

'Just like a shadow raptor,' Theodore whispered, remembering how silently they had crept up back on Aru.

'This filthy saur boy is with Logan, General,' Hayter called out. 'Where is your sister?'

Carter continued to rhythmically clap and walked

out into the centre of the circular clearing, so that it formed a green halo around him as he stood in the middle like a divine being.

Carter was well aware everyone and everything was staring at him. So he did something to make sure they all maintained their attention: he started to dance. But this was no ordinary dance – it was his shadow raptor dance.

Carter pulsated his arms in and out in time with his heartbeat. He arched and lowered his head, bending his knees as he did so. He slowed his movements so that they were big and wide, forcing all eyes to fixate upon his every move.

'He's milking the attention a bit,' said Theodore, who had seen the mesmerising display before.

'No,' Lucia said under her breath. 'The clever lad is buying Bea and Javier time – Look!' Lucia nodded towards the edge of the clearing.

As Carter was coming to the climax of his dance, everyone – the General, Hayter, the Doctor, Ash, Bishop, all the General's loyal guards, and all the farmers – watched as all around them adult brachios broke forth and entered the clearing. He splayed out his arms, which had once worn an array of feathers gathered from his clan, as he settled on the ground. He then raised himself up and stood tall, just like when he had first stood upright like a human in the clearing back on Aru. As he did this he raised his arms to the sky, and simultaneously all the brachios rocked backwards, lifting their forelimbs and raised themselves up onto their back legs.

It was a magnificently memorable spectacle. Time seemed to pass very slowly. Carter seemed to be holding the enormous saurs up by willpower alone until he started to lower his arms. The brachios followed his command, tilting forward, and as Carter quickly dropped his arms completely they all followed suit, crashing their legs down together onto the ground in one precise moment. It felt like a million drums beaten at exactly the same time, and it sent up a cloud of dust with such force that everyone fell backwards in shock.

The Doctor picked himself up and brushed himself down. In California he had seen Carter somehow emit a painful sound that stunned the tyrants and himself, but commanding saurs of this size and number was unbelievable. 'I wonder what's in his glands?' he muttered to himself.

Theodore's captor shoved another boot into his back, sending him to the ground again.

'Impressive,' the General said. 'But ultimately pointless. Señor Hayter, I asked you to do something for me. Why is it you're still standing there?'

Christian Hayter pulled his bullhook out from his belt loop and stepped over towards Buttercup, who could see what was about to happen, and cowered from him. Hayter patted the silver head of his weapon and

said, 'The hard way or the easy way – it's your choice.'
Buttercup stood still as he mounted her and, swinging
the Mountain Lythronax round, Hayter charged towards
the boy.

Carter stood his ground and observed with curiosity.
Back in California he and Theodore had both been chased
around a ghost town by Brown and Mountain Tyrants
controlled by the strange Doctor, and once again the
same man stood there on the sidelines looking at them
all through his round darkened glasses. It occurred to
Carter now that Hayter must have also been in America
with him but out of sight. Hayter had trained this tyrant
just like he had Buster.

Carter, unfazed by the man and saur charging towards
him, remained extraordinarily calm. He simply held out
one hand and then sharply forced it down, which brought
the Mountain Tyrant crashing to the ground. Hayter
tumbled off, righted himself, and in one fluid movement
went to swing his bullhook at Carter . . . and let out a
blood-curdling scream. Buttercup had also rolled over and
got quickly to her feet and bit straight down into Christian
Hayter's other shoulder. Everyone winced as the tyrant
lifted Hayter up and shook him violently like a rag doll,
making him drop his bullhook. Carter picked it up and
saw the new addition, a keystone embedded in the hilt. It
gave him an uneasy, ominous feeling, as if he was playing
cards against a loaded deck.

Buttercup dropped Hayter to the floor and dipped her head down and tugged at one of his legs, trying to get a good grip to lift him up again. Kicking and screaming loudly in great pain, he tried to beat away the Mountain Tyrant with his one good arm. Seeing the fresh blood soaking through his torn clothes and spurting from the deep lacerations, Carter stepped closer and let out a silent scream that stopped and momentarily froze the tyrant and all of the wild brachios in their tracks. Just as at the ghost town back in California the Doctor observed the boy take control with ease. Carter then pointed to the tyrant and dropped his hand to the ground, making it let go of Hayter's leg. The tyrant

nervously stepped back as Carter walked over and placed a hand on the Mountain Tyrant to reassure her he meant no harm. The saur shook herself down as Buster, who'd wrenched himself loose in the commotion, bounded over to them.

'Do something!' the General barked at the Doctor, who in turn motioned to Ash and Bishop. 'Unleash the Irritators!' he commanded.

Ash and Bishop were mesmerised like everyone else, and it took a second more insistent order before they jumped to the task. They scrambled past the farmers to the pen and unhooked the latch. Ash let out a whistle and instantly the smaller saurs became alert. Bishop pulled the knuckleduster from his pocket and held it high into the light so that it shone. Another whistle shrilled out and the pack of trained Irritators darted out and into the clearing.

'This will stop the boy,' said the Doctor with pride, but that was soon dissolved.

The Irritators trampled on top of Hayter to get to Carter, who held out his arms, and the Irritators

ran around, bouncing with joy and licking him like overexcited puppies. Buster behaved like a jealous dog and let out his rattle to ward them off. They didn't need further encouragement, fleeing past the circle of brachios and back into the jungle. Ash whistled as loud as he could, but they did not return.

The infuriated Doctor nodded at Bishop. 'Your turn,' he said coldly. Bishop looked down at his knuckleduster and handed it to the Doctor. 'Sorry.' He shook his head. 'You try.'

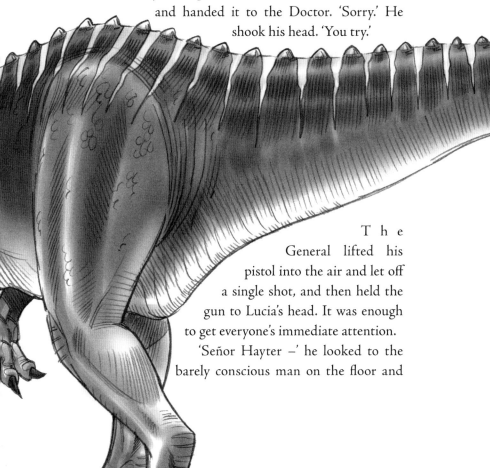

The General lifted his pistol into the air and let off a single shot, and then held the gun to Lucia's head. It was enough to get everyone's immediate attention. 'Señor Hayter –' he looked to the barely conscious man on the floor and drawled frustratedly – 'all this time I wondered how you controlled your tyrant. I asked myself how did Señores Ash and Bishop make the Irritators attack? What was the secret of your abilities? Yet here is a boy more powerful than all of you put together.' He shrugged. 'And here I am with just a humble firearm and it seems I'm the one still in control. This situation is over. My men don't just have the Viscount's eggs; they also have his guns – you know, the ones you thoughtfully supplied when you arrived. My men – my rebels, let's call them – have enough ammunition to win this stand-off several times over. It's time for you to back down and admit defeat.'

Carter stepped forward towards the General, and as he did so all the saurs followed. Javier appeared bareback on a brachio and pulled up alongside Carter. Its enormous bulk blocked out the sunlight and cast a dark shadow over the General and his frightened men. Crashing out from the dark dense jungle came Bea. Between every other brachio appeared a titanosaur. They all shook out their long extended spines, roared out loud at once, and thundered up close.

Bea, straddled round the lead titanosaur's huge head, stepped all the way forward to join Javier and her brother.

'You may have the guns,' Carter said, 'but I have my friend and big sister.'

27

The Gemini Festival Parade

~ twins ~

'Where is General Vulpez?' asked the president. 'He's missing the parade.'

The mayor puffed on his cigar. 'Probably on patrol looking out for the Rebels, Señor President,' he lied.

The Viscount glanced at his watch; the General was not the only person missing. He looked back past the white steps to the municipal building, where the procession passed by, and then out to the crowds of revellers who had gathered to watch. This was the best place to get a full view of the event. The entire route of the procession was visible, right from where it started a few streets away and wound into the central square, past where the Viscount stood, as it turned and left the square on the other side, finally working its way back to where it started.

People dressed in colourful costumes rode upon pairs of saurs of all kinds. The saurs themselves were decorated with brightly painted patterns and bore garlands of pom-poms on their reins and saddles. All ages were represented in the procession; old couples from their respective civic organisations rode gentle saurs, while children giggled upon small ones. Every now and then a single saur bore upon its back a pair of riders, who were themselves twins, to honour the festival's origins. These twins wore cloaks of jet black decorated with the Gemini constellation sewn in silver thread. The stars of Castor and Pollux featured little mirrors or sequins, which glinted brightly as they caught the sun. In between the riders groups of children skipped, tossing dried flowers from baskets into the crowd.

There was a commotion of sorts coming in the opposite direction that slowed down and then halted the procession. Everyone's heads turned like a wave to see what the cause was. The band playing nearby slowly quietened down as one by one the musicians also looked over.

'What now?' the president complained.

'It looks to be two people riding a brachiosaur, Señor President,' the police chief said, pointing out the long neck wafting above the crowds.

The president grumbled and leant forward to catch a glimpse. 'Strange markings,' he mused. 'What kind is that?'

The crowd parted as the brachio approached, and they could see it more clearly.

'It's been painted to look like a skeleton!' said the mayor.

'And something else . . .' The police chief stared. 'Are there two tyrants parading in front?' he said with alarm.

The Viscount suddenly took interest and craned to get a better look. Sure enough, the crowds were all parting for two tyrants – one black and heavily feathered, and the other golden and muscular. The Black Tyrant appeared to have white paint on it, depicting its skeleton. The Mountain Tyrant was marked with black paint in the same way.

'Strange decorations for a festival,' said the president. 'They look like opposite twins!' he exclaimed. 'Are they lost? The parade goes that way; two by two they pass every year the same. Everyone knows that. Why come the wrong way?' he complained.

'Tyrants are dangerous saurs to have around people,' fretted the police chief. 'This is most unusual and dangerous. Who's organising it this year?' He turned to an official standing close by looking puzzled at a clipboard.

'No tyrants on my list, Chief,' he said.

The Viscount leant in to the president. 'Sir, I apologise in advance for the momentary pause in today's proceedings,' he said, blushing a little with embarrassment. 'I'm not sure, but I believe they might be my guests arriving. They are unaware of the routine and normally only travel with the Black Dwarf Tyrant.'

The president looked startled.

'I can assure you he's well trained,' the Viscount assured him. 'So is the Mountain Tyrant.' The Viscount paused as he realised who was riding the saurs.

The mayor tapped the Viscount's elbow and gestured for him to step aside. 'That's Señor Hayter's tyrant,' he whispered, 'but he's not riding it. What's going on? Who is the girl?'

The Viscount shrugged his shoulders with a deeply concerned look on his face. What was Bea doing on Buttercup?

'What's painted on the sides of the army trucks following them?' asked the president, sounding increasingly alarmed.

The Viscount looked towards the two drab army trucks following the brachio and the tyrants. Adorning the sides, crudely painted in white, were two large tritop skeletons.

'Señor President,' the police chief said in alarm, 'it's Rebels! They look like the missing army trucks the Rebels stole from the dock last week!'

'Where is General Vulpez when you need him?' demanded the president, backing away up the steps, towards the door of the building behind.

The police chief signalled to some of his men and ran down the steps to face the oncoming visitors. He was uncomfortably aware, however, that should trouble break out his policemen were outnumbered.

✦ ✦ ✦

Bea and Carter were aware of the curiosity they were causing amongst the festival crowd. Everyone was giving the tyrants room, but tensions arose when the crowd became more tightly packed. No one wanted to run away, and everyone wanted to know who these people were. Never before had tyrants been paraded at the Gemini Festival, and no one had seen such unusual, sombre decorations on saurs before.

Finally Carter could see up the white steps to the municipal building and spotted Lambert standing next to someone who looked to be

of great importance, so he gave a little wave and smiled. Bea was also relieved to see Lambert and mouthed 'hello' to him. The police chief watched the Viscount politely wave back and gave a sigh of relief.

As they arrived the tyrants' and brachios' full body paint could be seen in all its splendour. Bea and Carter drew the tyrants to the left side of the steps, and Poppo Miguel with Javier moved Budge over to the right side, creating enough room for the two decorated army trucks to pull up side by side in the middle of the steps. Bea and Carter dismounted, and so did Javier.

'Well, the paint job certainly got everyone's attention,' Bea said to Javier. 'Let's tell them the good news.'

Before they could proceed an official came down the steps with his clipboard and held out his hand. 'This is a private area for ticket holders,' he said stiffly, clearly ill at ease with the situation but determined to do his job. Before the man could finish, Bea had handed over three tickets and the three of them pushed past and bounded up the steps, taking their places next to Lambert, before the president.

'Señor President, may I introduce my godson, Carter Kingsley, and his adorable sister Beatrice Kingsley,' Lambert said.

'And this is our friend, Javier Cantera,' said Bea, after they had bowed their heads. 'Forgive our intrusion, Mr President, but we have travelled from the jungle where we have made an important discovery we want to bring to your attention.' Bea paused, unsure whether everything she'd planned to say was coming out too fast. The Viscount coughed and went to tap her on the arm, but she shifted without looking at him and his hand fell short.

The president raised his eyebrows at her to continue, saying, 'And what might that be?'

Bea cleared her throat and continued. 'My brother and I – and Theo and our friends – have discovered an illegal tritop farm run by what appeared to be the Rebels,' she said in a rush. 'I believe they were plotting to disrupt today's event.'

'And, instead, you have disrupted it,' stated the president impatiently.

'Sorry.' Bea blushed.

'Tell me,' the president went on, 'how did you escape from these vile Rebels?'

'Señor President,' said Carter, jumping to his sister's aid, 'the people hiding in the jungle aren't Rebels – they are your very own army.'

'What?' the president spluttered.

'It's true, Señor President,' Javier spoke up. 'General Vulpez and his loyal guards have been dressing up as the Rebels and causing all of your problems.'

'You expect me to believe three children who turn up out of the blue telling tall stories?' the president scoffed. 'What is the meaning of this?' He turned to the Viscount, who stood speechless.

At that moment Theodore stepped out from behind the wheel of the army truck and signalled for Lucia to do the same from the truck she was driving. They pulled at the canvas that covered the vehicle's rear and revealed their hidden cargo. In Lucia's truck all of the General's guards were tied up, and in Theodore's truck, also bound, were General Vulpez, Christian Hayter, the Doctor, Ash and Bishop.

The crowd gasped.

'This can't be true!' shouted the president. 'Bring General Vulpez to me!'

Theodore grabbed the General by the arm and helped him roughly off the truck. The General was red in the face and spat on the ground in front of Theodore.

The police chief glared at the man who was once his friend. The General met his stare with a sorry look in return. 'It's not true,' he protested, 'it is they who are the Rebels!' He tugged at the ropes binding his hands behind his back. 'Please, there is no need for this indignity in front of my beloved president, untie me!'

'He is a cunning fox and will say anything to get out of this, señor,' warned Theodore. 'Do NOT untie him.'

'I am the one in charge here, not you, señor,' said the police chief.

He pulled a knife from his belt, spun the General around, and in one move cut the rope.

'Thank you, my friend,' the General said.

The chief nodded and unclipped his sidearm before leading him up the steps to the waiting president.

'General Vulpez, there had better be a very good explanation for this,' the president fumed.

The mayor, standing just behind the president, turned a shade paler and glanced at the Viscount nervously. With everyone watching the General dusted down his uniform, stood tall, saluted – and then spun round and snatched the police chief's pistol from his holster.

General Vulpez quickly turned to point his gun at the president. 'I should have done this a long time ago!' he said through gritted teeth.

28

The Last Brachio Saurman

~ your amazing gift ~

The sound of music, which just before had given the parade its festive spirit, screeched to an awkward halt, a single trumpet's note sputtering to a stop in the dusty air. The crowd held their breath at the sight of the General pointing the gun at the president.

Then the crowd gasped as one. A punk brachio was bounding up the steps towards the group, a rider on its back. The president looked past General Vulpez's shoulder and instinctively stepped backwards.

The General felt a cool shadow pass over his back. Before he could turn, the charging brachio had lowered its head and flipped him off his feet, high into the

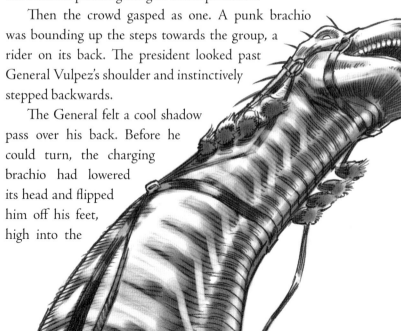

air, his arms and legs waving. A single shot rang out from the pistol the General had been holding, blasting the air with a crack, which was quickly followed by cries and screams as people twisted to see where it had come from and if they were in the firing line. The brachio quickly skidded to a halt, almost smashing into everyone else at the top, including Bea and Carter, just as the General landed with an almighty bone-cracking thud midway down the stone steps.

The president looked down in shock. He patted his chest in amazement.

'Are you hurt?' asked Bea.

To a collective sigh of relief the president gave a thumbs up. Everyone in the crowd started to cheer – not just for their president, but for the brachio and its heroic rider who had saved him.

The police chief was quickest to reach the General on the steps. He withdrew his pistol from Vulpez's broken hand and pulled him up roughly. 'We all saw what you did, traitor!' he announced loudly.

Lambert and Theodore ran over and winced when they saw the man's injuries. It was not just his wrist that appeared broken.

'Help me get rid of him,' the chief said.

The General cried out in pain as he was carried down the stairs and tossed into the back of the truck with the rest of his sorry-looking loyal guards.

'Take them away,' said the chief to one of his men.

Lambert tapped the police chief on the shoulder. 'These men require urgent medical attention,' he announced. 'Isn't it better to see to their injuries before an interrogation?' He pointed towards where the Doctor, Ash and Bishop sat with Hayter slumped over them, unconscious and bleeding. He paused and looked at Theodore standing beside him. 'Then they can face justice,' he explained.

'Certainly.' The police chief clicked his heels.

'Where shall I take them?' Theodore pulled the truck's keys from his pocket.

'No need for that,' said the mayor, who had joined them. 'My driver will take them to the medical centre.'

The president turned to Bea, Carter and Javier. 'I'm sorry I did not trust you,' he said. 'Thank you for foiling that traitor's plan and rounding them all up.' He gestured to Budge, still standing close by. 'The punk is with you?'

'Yes,' said Javier proudly, before Bea could reply. 'He is with us. His name is Budge.'

'So whom do I have to thank for riding this fine young

brachio named Budge?' the president asked.

They all turned towards Budge and saw at once that Poppo Miguel was no longer sitting upright, but had slumped over the brachio's neck. Blood ran from his shirt and trickled onto Budge's skin. As Lucia cried out in alarm, and ran towards her father-in-law, he slowly slid off the Budge's back. Javier rushed to catch him and he slumped into the arms of his family.

'Poppo!'

The bloodstain on his chest grew larger as they gently laid him down and knelt over him.

'Help!' the president cried out. 'A man's been shot!'

But as Javier held his grandfather he could tell it was too late. The life had finally left Poppo Miguel's body. Lucia picked up her father-in-law's limp hand and tried desperately to rub life back into its soft, well-worn grooves. But she too realised that his long time on the Earth was at an end, and that Poppo Miguel had passed on to another chapter, in the stars with Castor and Pollux.

Tears streamed down the faces of his family as grief overcame them.

Budge nudged the old man's lifeless body with his head, then turned to Javier, the saur pressing its weight into him.

'I know,' the boy sobbed, and patted Budge on the nose. 'I know.'

Bea held her hands to her mouth in shock. Carter knelt down beside Lucia and wept.

'What happened?' Theodore said, stunned, resting his hand on Lucia's shoulder, and he bit his lip as tears welled up in his eyes.

'Poppo and Budge saved the president,' said Lucia simply, 'but he was hit by the General's shot.'

The president reached down and put a hand on Javier's

shoulder. 'This man you loved is the nation's hero,' he said gravely. 'He saved my life and took the bullet that was intended for me.' The president knelt beside them. 'Was he your grandfather?' he asked in sombre tones.

Javier nodded, too overcome to speak.

'Poppo Miguel was the last Brachio Saurman,' Lucia wept.

'His sacrifice shall be honoured with a state funeral,' the president told them. 'Men like him made this country what it is today, and we must continue to honour their legacy as we move forward.'

Javier nodded but then spoke up. '*Gracias*, Señor President,' he said quietly but firmly. 'Thank you for your kind offer, but my grandfather would have wished to be buried at a resting place alongside his Saurmen ancestors. There is no need for any state ceremony.'

The president looked at the young man. 'As you wish,' he said respectfully.

Lucia stood and hugged her son. 'You're no longer my little boy,' she acknowledged proudly. 'You've grown to be just like your father.'

Javier turned to his mother. 'Thank you, Mama, but you are wrong about one thing.'

'Oh?' she replied, taken aback.

'Poppo Miguel wasn't the last Brachio Saurman,' Javier announced, standing tall. 'I am.'

✦ ✦ ✦

The silent crowd parted respectfully with bowed heads to let the stretcher carrying Poppo Miguel's body through, closely followed by Javier, Lucia, Bea, Carter, Theodore, Buster, Buttercup and Budge.

As they walked Bea pulled Javier to one side. 'I have something for you,' she said.

Javier looked at her quizzically.

'You can't be a Brachio Saurman without a brachiosaur,' Bea told him. 'And I happen to have one available. Budge is all yours,' said Bea.

'You're giving him to me?' Javier asked, surprised.

'I can't take him with me,' Bea said. 'We've got a long trip ahead of us, and besides – this is his home. Budge belongs with you. I've seen the connection you have with him. You can control him better than I ever did.'

'A punk of my own?' Javier said in amazement.

'You and your family have taught me so much and sacrificed everything. It's the least I can do,' Bea replied. 'Besides, it looks like Buster has a new friend,' she said, glancing over at the two tyrants who were walking closely together. 'We should take the Mountain Tyrant back to its home in California.'

'Bea, thank you from the bottom of my heart.' A smile lit up Javier's face. 'You are a true Saurwoman, just like Poppo said.'

29

Trust Me, I'm a Doctor

~ paths destined to cross ~

The army truck erratically clipped the last tree into the clearing and skidded to a halt by the hatchery, which was eerily void of any humans or saurs. Bishop hopped out of the driver's seat and ran round to the

back, opening the canvas door for the Doctor, who leapt down, while Ash missed his footing and fell to the ground.

'Grab your things – we're out of here in five minutes,' the Doctor snapped, then he paused, seeming to listen.

'What about the eggs?' asked Ash.

'Sssshhh!' The Doctor held a finger to his lips to shut him up. '*Verdammt!*' he spat furiously. 'The generators are silent – the heaters aren't on!' He ran inside the hatchery swearing in German.

Bishop looked round. 'The coast is clear; all the farmers have gone. How's the boss doing?'

Ash shook his head. 'Not good – he's unconscious.' He gestured to the back of the truck. 'Doc said he had something to help him recover and make him ten times better than before, though.'

They followed the Doctor into the hatchery where he was leaning against a post, sobbing. Some of the eggs had cracks where hatchlings had started to poke themselves out but were not able to finish the task; from one a tiny claw poked through, resting on the cold shell.

'All ruined!' he cried out. 'Come – there is nothing here for us now.'

'Oh yes there is,' said Bishop craftily.

A few minutes later, the three men were heaving a large packing crate that had once contained eggs into the back of the truck alongside Hayter, who was still out cold on the floor and soaked in his own blood.

'The Viscount will be very happy with his precious titanosaur skull,' the Doctor reasoned, climbing into the back to check on his patient.

'Hopefully he'll reward our efforts,' said Ash as he joined him.

The truck's engine kicked into gear and moved off with a jolt.

'You sure that you can fix the boss up, Doc?' asked Ash. 'He doesn't look good.'

The Doctor smiled, pulled out a vial of liquid that he had extracted from the titanosaur's glands and filled a large syringe. He held it up and flicked it a few times before jabbing it into Hayter's lacerated shoulder and plunging the contents into his bloodstream.

'Trust me,' he murmured, 'I'm a doctor.'

◆ ◆ ◆

Bea glared at Theodore, as angry as she had ever been in her life. 'What do you mean, Hayter's not at the hospital?' she demanded, hands on her hips.

'He never arrived,' Theodore told her, his arms crossed tightly across his chest.

'That horrible doctor – and the others?' Carter asked.

Theodore shook his head. 'All of them, gone.'

'How?' Bea and Carter said together.

'The mayor's driver was found halfway up the road,' Theodore explained. 'Apparently he was overpowered and kicked out of the vehicle, according to Lambert.'

'Hayter, that rat – how does he keep getting away?' Bea cried. 'Let's go after them – they can't be far, and Hayter's wounded. Someone will have seen them!' She spun round to get up on Buttercup, but Theodore grabbed her arm.

'Not this time, Bea,' he warned. 'Let him run.'

'What are you saying?' Bea gasped. 'Theodore, we can't let Hayter get away – we'll never catch him again!'

Theodore sighed. He understood her anger. 'Bea, do

you remember what the Stegosorcerer told me, when he arrived with all the saurs at Bunty's funeral?' he asked quietly. 'He said that our paths are destined to cross again, mine and Hayter – the bad man.'

'But they just did, Theodore,' Bea cried, 'and you're letting him get away! He killed Grandma, remember!' Her anger was at boiling point. Why would Theodore betray Bunty like this?

Theodore rested the palm of his hand on the keystone set in the hilt of his blade as he chose his words carefully.

'I'm not so sure that's the truth any more,' he told her. 'I'm not sure we know much of the truth to be honest.'

'What do you mean?' asked Carter, shocked.

'The fire that killed Bunty,' Theodore stated firmly.

Bea corrected him. 'But Hayter locked her in the basement. He *let* the fire kill her. Theodore, you know he did!'

Theodore shook his head. 'What we know is that Bunty – that loving and kind-hearted woman – went into a burning house to free Hayter.' Theodore paused for thought. 'But someone else could have locked her in there.'

'What are you saying?' Bea shouted. 'Have you gone mad? HAYTER DID IT!'

Theodore shook his head more firmly. 'I hate that horrid little man as much as you do,' he told them. 'He's done unspeakable things and bragged about them all. So why is it that when I'm tied up, defenceless and at his mercy, he denied killing her?' Theodore paused to let it sink in. 'Why lie? Why pretend he didn't kill her?'

Before Bea could object again, Theodore pressed on. 'Hayter had me tied up, just like I had him tied up in the very basement in which Bunty perished, but rather than tell me something that would hurt me – rather than remind me of the moment he tricked her, say, or when he pushed her back inside the basement she'd freed him from, or the moment he turned the key in the lock sealing her fate – he *denied* it. He was adamant.'

'He was messing with your head, Theo,' Bea said firmly.

'That may be so,' Theodore replied, 'but I'm not having the blood of someone who could be innocent on my hands, even if it is Christian Hayter.'

Bea stamped her foot, just like her grandmother would have done. 'Pull yourself together, Theo!'

'But if Hayter didn't do it, then who did?' Carter asked.

'He said he wasn't the only person inside the house at the time,' Theodore said.

'So who else was in the house?' said Bea. 'No one!'

'Lambert was,' Carter said quietly.

Theodore and Bea turned to face him. 'No, Carter – Lambert was outside. He ran in to pull me out,' Theodore said.

Carter shook his head sadly. 'He was inside the house before that.'

'Hayter killed Grandma,' Bea said forcefully. 'Think

of it – why would Lambert, who has no reason to –'

'But that's just it,' Theodore stopped her. 'Neither does Hayter. No one had a reason to kill Bunty.'

They were silent in thought before Theodore concluded, 'Things just don't add up.' He sighed. 'Hayter's up to his eyeballs in *something* and there's a reason he keeps turning up and ruining our lives. He's not just after getting Buster back and settling grudges with me. There's something bigger going on – and we need to find out what that is. No doubt he's lying about Bunty, but we need to find out why he'd bother.'

'Maybe we're not being told the truth about a lot of things,' Carter remarked. 'My parents being killed by the clan of shadow raptors, for example. I don't believe it. Poppo Miguel told me to look inside myself. I know those raptors – they raised me. They just would not have done that.'

'But Carter –' Bea stopped mid-sentence, unsure of what to say next, but deeply worried and still angry at Hayter's escape.

'I promise you both, Bea and Carter,' Theodore assured them, 'whoever locked Bunty in the basement will get what's coming to them. We will bring them to justice.' Theodore stood tall. 'For now, we must try to lead something like a normal life – whatever that is.'

30

Treasured Memories

~ memories of treasure ~

Javier led the small funeral for Poppo Miguel back at the brachio nest and everyone was surprised to see new sets of eggs laid there. The other punks had been led away and the three *abuelas* patiently waited for the next brood to hatch. On their way back to the village, Theodore, Bea, Carter, Lucia and Javier returned to the site of the lost city to find the new cutting had shot up, ensuring that the entrance was well and truly lost to all but Saurmen.

The Canteras were rewarded with a new home near the site of their old one, courtesy of the grateful president, and Lucia was given a job working to preserve the land from poachers, which suited her perfectly. Javier learnt to ride Budge in expert fashion, and eventually took up his role not as a Brachio Herder but a Brachio Saurman, keeping the brachios from entering the villages, and the villagers from entering the jungle, just as generations of Saurmen had done before him.

Lambert was visibly shocked to hear from Theodore

that crates from his Sauria Firearms Corporation had
been used to convey tritop eggs to an illegal hatchery. To
make up for this terrible slur on his reputation he brokered
a trade deal with the government to allow them to import
SPAW at a greatly reduced rate.

Bea produced a number of sketches of the jewelled
titanosaur skull from memory, helped along by her
remarkable photographs. The president vowed to find the
important artefact, which had disappeared along with the
wanted fugitives Doctor Achteka and Christian Hayter,
and their henchmen who were known to the authorities
only as Ash and Bishop.

Buster and Buttercup became inseparable, and
Theodore insisted they accompany the Mountain
Lythronax back to live on Cash Kingsley's ranch in
California, her native territory.

♦ ♦ ♦

How far they'd come, Bea mused, and how far they still
had to go. She closed her eyes, popped the remains of a
fried *chapuline* she'd found in her pocket into her mouth,
and started humming a lullaby that came from the heart,
but belonged to all time.

♦ ♦ ♦

THE END

Excerpts from
Saurs of the Wild

~ *by Nigel Winsor* ~

Editor's note: Extracts from the
updated 2012 edition of
Saurs of the Wild, with further
material by Philip Winsor

AMARGAS

Herbivore | Quadruped

Amargas are only nine metres long as an adult and follow
the typical sauropod body shape, with a long tail and neck;
a small head with a horse-like broad snout equipped with
pencil-like teeth; and a barrel-shaped trunk supported by
four column-like legs, each with five toes, the inner digit
being the longest. They are known for the distinctive rows
of spines down their neck and back, which are taller than

in any other known sauropod. Fossils show that some members of the family had a keratinous sheath covering the extended vertebrae, which added significantly to the total length of the spines and was probably used to defend against larger predators. The tallest spines reach on average 60cm on the eighth cervical disc. These help members of the social herd identify each other, even in their dense forested habitat. The two parallel rows of spines provide a scaffold that supports a skin sail, which is used for display and combat between competing males. Patterns and markings on the sails are like fingerprints that otherwise distinguish the relatively androgynous bodies of both male and female amargas.

At rutting season, males fill their neck sails with blood to attract a suitable mate. This also causes short bouts of aggression towards other males, each fighting for

dominancy. Once the short mating season is over, calm and order soon resume. Both parents care for the offspring through infancy in equal measure, further entrenching the apparent androgyny of these saurs.

Being considerably smaller than other sauropods, amargas can live alongside other larger species and exploit different food sources in order to reduce competition. Most often they can be found living alongside Yucatan Brachios, the largest of the brachio species, eating low foliage, ferns and grass that the brachios can't reach. Deforestation and the reduction in suitable habitat is believed to have caused the extinction of many diminutive saur ancestors, and unless something can be done to preserve the remaining wild population of amargas, these too will soon become endangered.

BRACHIOS
Herbivore | Quadruped

Brachios are a distinctive group of sauropods with disproportionately long necks, short tails, steeply inclined trunks and small heads with a large brow bump. Unlike most sauropods, brachios' forelimbs are longer than their hind limbs, resulting in their sloping body. They have five-toed forefeet with a single claw on the first toe, and three-toed hind feet with claws on each toe. Their robust wide muzzles and thick jaws with spoon–shaped

teeth allow them to strip foliage easily. Their long necks mean that they prefer to feed on foliage well above the ground, but many are known to also strip away at low-lying shrubs when taller trees are scarce. Brachios carve long grooves in the ground with their feet and lay a line of eggs in communal nesting sites. The partially buried eggs are guarded by elderly females, which also take on the role of rearing the infants. Reducing the number of adults around the nesting sites helps to sustain enough vegetation for the remaining guardians to eat.

There are four types of brachios, identified by the landmass they originate from. The Indian Brachio is most common, as it is the smallest and simplest to train. The biggest of the brachios is the South American or Latin Brachio. Spanish conquistadors looted eggs as well as gold, and introduced them to Europe. This resulted in African and Indian

Brachios interbreeding. The African Brachio differs from the other types of brachios in three ways: they have a longer and thicker neck set into bulkier shoulders and a higher brow bump. In appearance, the African Brachio looks remarkably like a cross between a giraffe and an elephant, and is the largest creature to dominate the continent. The large nasal cavity within its brow bump allows sound to resonate, and its cry can be heard for miles around. Surprisingly African Brachios are great swimmers and will swim miles around the coast to get to lush grazing sites. They can often be found cooling down in waterholes and enjoying mud baths. The only true pure-breed brachios left in the world are the Yucatan Brachio, a small population of which resides in the dense jungles that link Mexico, Guatemala and Belize. The fossil record shows that brachios previously enjoyed a wider global territory, but today they can only be found in the lush forests of Central America.

During their adolescent years, 'punk' brachios are well known for their unruly behaviour. The subculture and music movement popular in the mid 1970s and 1980s in Great Britain, America and Australia, derives its name from these young 'punk' brachios. In addition, punk brachios sport long keratin spines down the centre of their heads, and this is thought to be an inspiration for the distinctive Mohawk (or Mohican) hairstyle associated with punk rockers, where both sides of the head are shaved, leaving the noticeably longer hair in the centre to be spiked. This hairstyle can in fact be dated back over 2,000 years: the Clonycavan Man, a 2,000-year-old male body discovered in a bog near Dublin, Ireland in 2003, was found to be wearing Mohawk-styled hair straightened with plant oil and pine resin. The indigenous people of North America who originally inhabited the Mohawk Valley in upstate New York did not shave their heads but rather pulled their hair out, small tufts at a time, to create a square of hair on the back of the crown of the head that was then formed into three braids and decorated. The "Mohawk" or "Mohican" hairstyle is more common among the Pawnee people, who historically lived in present day Nebraska and in northern Kansas.

RUBEOSAURS

Herbivore | *Quadruped*

These quadrupeds have a thin tail and short weak limbs with three hooves on each forefoot, and four hooves on each hind foot. Often mistaken for styracos, rubeos have an impressively large nose horn that is wide and curves upwards at the end, with four elongated horns at the top of their thin bony frills. The frill has two symmetrical abstract patches that look like a Rorschach inkblot test. Rubeo hides range in colour from grey to petrol-blue with pale and dark patches over them in a random distribution. Males are bright yellow in colour, with females a paler cream.

Rubeo eggs and meat are bitter to taste and unsuitable for humans, and their hides too thick and wrinkled to be of any practical use. One reason why these saurs have survived alongside other attractive, tastier, stronger and more practical ceratops is that their nose horn has become a desirable object for a growing tourist industry. Now found only in Central America, these saurs perform duties for owners who cannot afford harder-working ankylos whilst they are young, and once their nose horns reach a suitable size they are slaughtered. The rest of the saur is sold as cheap food for carnivorous saurs held in captivity.

SPINOSAURS

Carnivore | Biped

These semi-aquatic theropods stand out from other top predators around the world. All members of the spinosaur family share distinctive crocodile-like heads, having a curved snout with a kink and a thin jaw fixed on a strong neck and slender body, with strong forearms with three clawed fingers. Their legs and the height of their neural spines, however, differs through the family. Spinosaurs have no feathers; instead they have evolved to have thin layers of keratinous scales and spines that moult and are replaced easily. This gives them a flexible and waterproof layer over their skin, making them more like Komodo dragons than semi-aquatic saurs that have waterproof feathers, such as the Dwarf Black Tyrant.

Members of the spinosaur family can be found close to water across the world, around coastlines, inlets and lakes. The largest of the species, Spinosauri, is also known to spend long periods in open water. Like tyrants, these carnivores are formidable hunters. They feed predominantly on fish from both saltwater and fresh water, thanks to extra-sensory receivers in their distinctively curved snout. By dipping their snout in the water they can detect fish and manoeuvre themselves into position, before selecting the perfect moment to snap up their next meal in their powerful jaws. Their long conical teeth have smooth edges and are suitable for grabbing and holding prey. These differ from the teeth of other theropods, which are serrated, and better suited to tearing or dismembering body parts. Their nostrils are positioned far to the rear of their heads, and their secondary palate makes respiration possible even if the majority of the jaw is under water.

All spinosaurs will take the opportunity to eat other small prey apart from fish, and the smallest of the species, the Irritator, has now been split into two sub-species due to a new population that prefers to remain inland, having adapted their extra-sensory ability for hunting and now primarily consuming rodents.

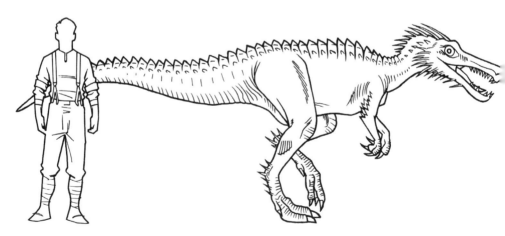

Irritators (Inferior Land & Intelligent Coastal)

Irritators, as their name suggests, often present more of an irritation than a concern to humans. Falling short of their heritage, they are known for not being the smartest of carnivores, even mocked in popular children's rhymes as the 'scared saur who does not realise it's a carnivore'.

However, Irritators and their close family were once very much feared by fishermen around the world and it has been observed that Irritators living near the coast remain more like their other family members, whereas Irritators that have taken up residence away from the sea often behave completely differently. For the most part, it is the inland Irritators who humans come into contact with, hence their reputation. 'Inferior Land' Irritators have in recent years been considered in some circles to be a separate species from the newly named 'Intelligent Coastal' Irritators. This reclarification of the species remains controversial; if Coastal Irritators and Land Irritators breed they produce fertile offspring so cannot yet be considered to be a separate species and thus we do not list them as such in this publication. The outcome of this fiercely debated argument may only be settled after many more years of separation between these two types of saur. Both sub-species still look identical, with large diamond-shape patches down the spine leading to thin stripes in tones of bright and lime green. Males have bright patches of cobalt blue and yellow around the eyes, and females an almost fluorescent pink.

Scientists and biologists have for a long time debated why this division between the coastal-dwelling and inland Irritators might have arisen. The established theory puts it down to the proximity of the inland Irritators habitat in Central America to the world's largest and most feared predator, the Tyrannotitan. However, recent studies now suggest this adaptation has been caused by a radical change in their diet. Inland Irritators live in locations where most of the waterways lie underground. Their traditional diet of fish is limited, only accessible via sinkholes in the limestone. Irritators have quickly adapted, using their sensory snouts to snuffle out rodents, and, in some instances, ground-nesting birds, proving that these saurs are resourceful and adaptable. This change in diet has contributed to the lack of omega-3, which would otherwise have been found in fish. Where this occurs, inland Irritators can seem timid and behave more like herbivores than carnivores.

TYRANNOTITAN
Carnivore | Biped

The Tyrannotitan is one of the largest known terrestrial carnivores, with fully grown adults usually measuring up to 13 metres long. Despite its common name of Titanic Tyrant, it belongs in the allosaur family. Tyrannotitans have three formidable claws on their forelimbs, whereas all tyrants have just two claws. Other distinctive characteristics include large eyes; a narrow skull; the thigh (femur) being longer than the shin (tibia), making it unable to run as fast as a tyrant; and extended neural spines over the hip, which give them a distinctive humped, rather than flat, back.

Solitary by choice, male and female Tyrannotitans only tolerate each other for short breeding seasons. Unlike many species, there is no competitiveness between males during mating season. They have evolved to avoid aggression towards each other and will avoid conflict by moving off. It could be said that this has preserved their numbers; being the top predator means the only thing that could harm a Tyrannotitan is another Tyrannotitan. Both sexes have vertical stripes – a good form of camouflage for their habitat – in a variety of unusually bright colours. To the human eye they stand out, but to the reduced colour vision of their prey they almost dissolve into the background.

Although tyrants have historically been considered the largest living theropods, in fact the Tyrannotitan is often roughly equal in size. Some researchers even argue that they should be classified as larger than tyrants as their body mass is bigger and their extended neural spines make them taller. Compared side by side with the African White Titan Tyrant, which can grow to be almost 14 metres long but has a slender build, the Tyrannotitan still looks a lot bigger due to its larger build, baggier skin and taller neural spines. Interestingly they weigh on average the same, with the tyrants' dense muscle and wide skull making up the weight.

Tyrannotitans, as members of the allosaur family, are genetically older than tyrants and have remained relatively unchanged for millions of years. Their reclusive lifestyle and habitat in the dense jungles of Central and Southern America keeps them well away from mankind. However, the deforestation of these ancient jungles has reduced their numbers considerably. No exact count has ever been made, but it is estimated that there are perhaps only fifty breeding pairs left. Like the extinct Giganotosaur, the largest of all theropods famously wiped out by Spanish conquistadores, whose sad skeletal remains fill museums around the world, many people fear that these huge majestic Tyrannoritans will soon die out too.